I0607962

Ocean Floors

From the Tales of Dan Coast

Ocean Floors

From the Tales of Dan Coast

By

Rodney Riesel

Published by Island Holiday Publishing

East Greenbush, NY

ISBN: 978-0-997-1149-5-9

Second Edition

Cover Design & Maps by:

Connie Fitsik

To learn about my other books friend me at

https://www.facebook.com/rodneyriesel

For Brenda

Kayleigh, Ethan,

&

Peyton

KEY LARGO

N E S W

ISLAMORADA

MARATHON

BIG PINE KEY &
THE LOWER KEYS

KEY WEST

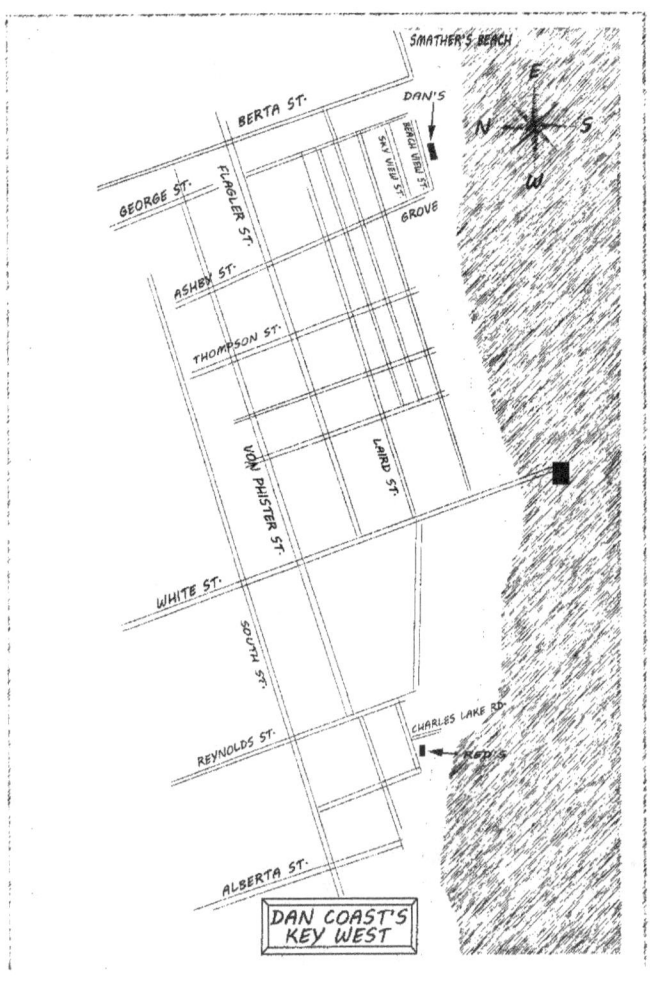

SMATHER'S BEACH

BERTA ST.

DAN'S

GEORGE ST.

FLAGLER ST.

SKY VIEW ST.

GROVE

ASHBY ST.

THOMPSON ST.

VON PHISTER ST.

LAIRD ST.

WHITE ST.

SOUTH ST.

REYNOLDS ST.

CHARLES LAKE RD.

KEN'S

ALBERTA ST.

DAN COAST'S
KEY WEST

Inside every child's mind,

You never know

What you will find.

Their own world of creativity,

Imagination is their reality

~ Peyton Riesel

Chapter One

Dan Coast opened his eyes to the sound of a naked woman looking for her underwear. Whatever that sound might be. She was forty, maybe forty-five. Who knows these days? Every woman under sixty tries to look twenty. Her skin was tanned. Not too tanned. No tan lines. She was holding a pair of faded jeans, the kind with pre-made, thread bare holes. Twenty-five years ago she probably wore a pair just like them to a Bon Jovi, or Poison concert. Ten years ago she would have scoffed at any woman wearing a pair. Now, doing as the magazines and the Style Network have told her, she's wearing them again.

Draped over her left forearm she had a white wife beater, probably not Hanes, or Fruit of the Loom. Hollister probably, or American Eagle. Whichever store made her feel younger that day. Whichever store had a young good looking sales clerk who was smart enough to say, "Wow, forty? Really? You don't look forty. I would have guessed twenty-eight, maybe twenty-nine."

In the same hand she had a pair of pink Adidas sneakers. Running shoes. From the looks of those toned legs, she used those running shoes quite a bit. She walked around the carpet on her tip-toes, which made the muscles in her calves stand out. *Nice*, Dan thought.

With the other arm she was doing her best to cover her large, fake, tanned breasts.

Great job on the boobs, Dan thought.

There was a slight scar underneath each breast. He hadn't noticed that last night, but then again with the amount of tequila that was consumed he probably wouldn't have noticed a conjoined twin hanging off the front of her.

Dan looked around the room without moving his head. He was lying on his stomach, his head turned to the side so he could watch his naked guest. His legs were sticking out from the bottom of the sheet, and his feet hung over the edge of the bed.

Nice room, he thought. Not the best he had been in, but surely better than the one they would be in if he himself had footed the bill. The room was furnished with real wood furniture. Not the kind that looks like it was constructed out of recycled kitchen countertops. There was dark blue carpeting, shag. Dan remembered how the carpet felt on his bare feet, and his knees, and his back the night before. Dan grinned. He was glad shag carpeting had come back in fashion for a while. The walls were painted a soft, light blue, and the moldings were oversized. Pine probably. They were painted off-white. *Cozy*. There was a night stand on each side of the bed, each with a matching lamp. A forty-two inch plasma television beckoned atop the dresser. *It would be nice if she left now so I could watch some TV,* Dan thought groggily. *Hey wasn't this the week Me-TV was going to have that* Magnum PI *marathon?*

"Where's my bra and panties?" the naked lady demanded furiously, shooting him a disgusted look.

Dan didn't answer. He just lay there enjoying the show, and wondered why she was making such an attempt to cover up those beautiful breasts. After all, there was no part of her he hadn't seen just a few short hours before. Another thing, why did she choose to cover up the breasts and not the lower, well-groomed goodies? Women always make out that it's more taboo to see the lower than the upper, but when faced with the decision, they always seem to cover the upper. After all, on this particular specimen, it was the lower section that told the hidden truth. She wasn't really blonde, she was a red head. *Carpet don't match the drapes,* Dan thought. He was grinning on the inside. It was probably best at this point that she not see him smiling.

"Can you help me? God! What was I thinking? This was a mistake," she cried out.

Ouch! Mistake? Dan thought.

"...and you better erase those pictures from last night, Coast."

Dan was smiling on the outside now. He remembered his camera on the night stand. He remembered the manila envelope containing the pictures he was paid two weeks earlier to take. He also remembered the few photos he took in the room last night. He took those for free.

From his vantage point, Dan could see the pink thong underwear beneath the dresser, and he remembered throwing the matching bra behind the head board during the frantic disrobing frenzy, but after the *mistake* remark he wasn't about to reveal their locations. *Screw her,* he thought. Dan wondered if this might be a good time to play the "You're getting warmer, you're getting colder" game. He decided against it.

Sure, there were mistakes made during the evening, he thought. Drinking way too much tequila, banging his client, eating the cotton balls he must have eaten at some point during the night. But he never would have said *mistake* out loud. Dan pulled the pillow over his head. *Ahhhh, nice and cool*. It's funny how a nice cool pillow feels so good on a hangover forehead. He drifted off.

Coast awoke again. He wondered how much time had gone by. The woman was gone. The panties were gone. The bra probably was too. He was alone in the room; still face down on the bed, spread eagle. The clock said nine-fifty. Check out is ten. *Crap! So much for enjoying Magnum, Higgins, and T.C. on the wide screen*, he thought.

He sat up and swung his legs over the side of the bed. He scrunched up his toes on the blue shag carpeting, stood, and walked slowly to the bathroom, his knees and ankles sounding like a Rice Crispies commercial. In the bathroom he got rid of some tequila. He opened his travel bag and looked for his toothbrush. Brushed his teeth and showered.

After dressing Dan returned to the bedroom. His camera was on the night stand. The manila envelope containing the pictures of fire crotch's husband and his secretary were gone. A small stack of eight, one hundred dollar bills lay in its place. *At least she paid me,* he thought. *It couldn't have been that big of a mistake.* He counted the money. *No tip.* Dan grinned and stuffed the money in his pants pocket.

Chapter Two

Dan Coast was about an hour and a half out of Miami, on US-1. *Take the Weather with You* was in the CD player, and Dan was singing along with "Bama Breeze," his favorite Buffett song. He pulled off onto the old highway in Islamorada. He had seen the billboard a few days earlier on his way to Miami. It was an old faded billboard. The kind two men must have put up with two brooms, a bucket of wallpaper paste, and a rickety old ladder. Not the new type of billboard, printed on a giant tarp and stretched across a sheet of three-quarter-inch plywood, held tight in the back with some kind or ratcheting tie-down.

Dan wondered how the Three Stooges could have gotten in any trouble at all stretching a tarp across plywood. No, he was sure the old type of billboard was the best.

This particular billboard had a picture of a giant flamingo wearing a chef's hat. He had a name tag that read "Sid." Above his head was a speech balloon that read, "All our steaks are Flame-mingo broiled." Corny yeah, but original.

Dan had seen the billboard on several trips up and down US-1. The billboard was for a little bar and grill that he had never tried before, but had always wanted to. It just never seemed to be dinner time, or lunchtime, when he passed through, and Sid's didn't serve breakfast. After all, who in their right mind would want flame-mingo broiled eggs? On this particular trip from Miami to Key West, Dan was passing through at lunchtime. His stomach rumbled, hankering, he guessed, for some of Sid's cooking.

It was cloudy, dark black and gray clouds. There was a mist in the air, and it looked like at any minute there could be a down pour. Not only did Coast's Porsche have just one working door, but it also had just one working wind shield wiper. The working wiper was on the driver side, and that's all Dan usually needed. How many days does it rain in paradise anyway? The windshield wiper on the passenger side was non-existent and the wiper arm sliding across the windshield made a noise like two banshees in a screaming match. The noise didn't usually bother him too much, but with almost two hours left of his trip home, and a possibility of rain, he figured it was more than he could take.

He pulled off of the road and into the parking lot of Sid's Beach Bar and Grill. He leaned over and opened the glove box. He reached in and shuffled through some papers, finally pulling out a small roll of duct tape. Some of the papers fell out onto the floor of the car. Dan picked them up. There were different types of papers with letterheads, and an assortment of pamphlets. One heading read, "Miami-Phillips Career College, Investigative Training." Another read "Get Your Associates Degree in Private Investigations," and a third read, "You Can Be A Private Detective." Dan looked at the papers, arranged them in a neat stack, and placed them back in the glove box.

Dan walked around to the passenger side of the car. Pulling the wiper away from the windshield, he took about a foot of duct tape and wound it around the tip in a clock wise motion about five or six times, and folded over the excess tape at the end. He walked back around to the driver's side, reached in and turned the key one click. He then turned on the wind shield wipers, and listened as they moved back and forth across the wind shield. There was almost no noise.

"All fixed," Dan said to no one, and grinning to himself. He started to put the top up, looked at the sky, and decided against it.

As Dan looked up, he noticed a man sitting in a rocking chair on the porch of the bar and grill, to the left of the front door. The man appeared to be in his late seventies. He was wearing a black satin vest over a long sleeved, pale blue and white striped shirt with a button down collar. He wore black jeans and flip-flops. His unshaven face was shaded by a small tan hat he wore cocked to one side. The man reminded Dan of a Vincent van Gogh self-portrait he had once seen in a museum, while on vacation with his wife. He stood and stared at the man for a moment, and then started walking across the dirt parking lot toward the door.

A life-sized porcelain statue of Sid the Flamingo, with a WELCOME sign dangling from his curved bill, greeted him at the bottom of the steps leading up to the entrance. The building was two stories with split slab siding, painted red, with a light gray steel roof. A front porch ran the entire width of the building, with the same steel roof. There were four round posts holding up the porch roof, with two square railings between each pole. There were four windows across the front of the second story, all with shutters, and curtains. All the curtains were the same, red and white checkered. The shutters were green. Dan thought the building looked more like a camp

17

in the Adirondacks, than an island bar and grill. It's usually places like this that weren't put together with tourists in mind. It was probably frequented by locals. The prices would be cheaper, and the food would be better.

"Judging from your unique abilities with an automobile, I'm guessing you must be a mechanic," the old man said to Dan. The old geezer spat something black and viscous in the dirt that looked like a mixture of Coke and 40-weight oil and then wiped the back of his hand across his chin.

The man remained completely straight faced, but the tone of his voice told Dan, he was making a joke. Dan laughed.

"No, I'm just an ordinary duct tape technician," Dan responded.

The old man grinned as Dan breezed past him into the bar.

Dan Coast removed his sunglasses, hung them on the front of his shirt, and walked through the swinging cafe doors slowly, the way one usually enters a place for the first time. He held both doors open momentarily as he stood between them, letting his eyes adjust to the darkness inside. Everyone in the room looked over. At that moment Dan felt a little foolish, realizing that he must have looked like someone doing a bad impression of John Wayne, casing the room for black hats before entering the saloon.

I wish I had that entrance to do over again, Dan thought. But then he thought, *I bet most people enter the same way.* He thought about doing Wayne's famous waddle across the floor, but refrained.

The interior walls were rough-cut pine. On two walls the pine ran horizontal, and on the other two it ran vertical. The boards were stained dark. The ceiling was high and covered in the same pine, but a lighter stain. Six fans hung from the ceiling, swishing in a lazy rhythm. The fans were all connected by one drive belt that ran to a centrally located motor. On the wall to the right was a jukebox, one of those space age-looking Wurlitzers with the cool bubble tubes running around the outside of the cabinet. Above it, mounted to the wall, were a bear head and an elk head looking bored and very dead. Patsy Cline's twangy voice boomed out from the jukebox on "I Fall to Pieces." A chunky barfly long past her prime swayed to the music in a lonely corner. Dan was home sick. He thought about Old Forge. He thought about Piseco Lake. He thought about his home in Up-state New York. He thought about his wife. Dan quickly shook off the feelings of nostalgia, and let the doors close behind him.

There were no booths, only tables, about nine of them, four chairs at each. Three tables were occupied. At one table there was a family, husband, wife, two kids. Two young men in their twenties were at another table, and at the third was a couple, probably in their mid-fifties.

The sign by the door read, "Please be seated anywhere," and that's what he did.

A gentleman behind the bar watched Dan as he crossed the room and sat. The man was wearing sunglasses indoors. Dan wondered why people did that. *Must be a fan of Howard Stern or Roy Orbison,* Dan thought. Dan was a big fan of both Orbison and Stern, but he never wore sunglasses indoors. That move should be saved for geniuses, and the blind.

The bartender wore a blue Hawaiian shirt. The first three buttons were undone, revealing what looked to be a gorilla suit underneath. His thinning black hair was slicked back tight against his scalp. His face was wide and simian, with a friendly, gap-toothed grin. His kinky hair, dark and greasy, grew in a widow's peak, and he had a tennis ball sized bald spot on his crown. He reminded Dan of a seedier version of Ernest Borgnine, and he thought there was something vaguely sinister, brutal even, behind the amiable exterior.

He was a big man, not tall, just big. He was about five-nine or ten. His shoulders were wide, and leaning on the bar with his arms stretched out as he was, he took up half the bar. His hands were large with short thick fingers. On three of the fingers and one thumb he wore rings. On his pinky was an onyx ring with a diamond in the center. The other rings just appeared to be plain gold and silver colored bands. Tangled in the man's chest hair was a thick gold chain with a gold razor blade hanging at the end.

"Someone will be right over, pal. Can I get you something to drink while you're waiting?" said the bartender.

"Tequila, Seven and lime." Dan said.

"I have Sprite, is that okay?"

"Sure." Dan shrugged.

The bartender made Dan's drink quickly, and brought it right over.

"Here ya go, pal," the bartender said.

"Thanks."

Dan wondered if this was Sid. He wasn't wearing the name tag, or the chef's hat. His legs wear too thick, and he didn't have that orange hue like most flamingos. *Must not be Sid*, Dan thought. *I wonder if the steaks are still flame-mingo broiled?*

The bartender walked back behind the bar, and through a swinging door, to what Dan assumed was the kitchen. He heard the man call out to someone named Paula, telling her she had another table. After a few seconds a woman exited the swinging door, tying an apron around her waist. Her nose was in the air, and her mouth was set in a line so straight, it might have been drawn with a ruler. As she walked by the bar she snatched up a pad of guest checks and approached Dan's table. One of the young men at the table of two looked toward the young woman. With his foot he quickly nudged his friend under the table. Both men stared as she stalked in Dan's direction. The bartender shot them a reproving look and they quickly returned to their meals.

"How are you today sir I'm Paula I'll be your server have you decided what you would like or do you need some more time," the girl said quickly, in one long monotone sentence, as she looked over toward the bartender, who was watching her, with eyes squinted and lips pursed. She looked back at Dan and with her right hand pulled her hair back behind her ear, revealing a small cut over her eye, and a small purple crescent-shaped mark under the eye.

By the way the bartender and waitress stared at each other, it was evident that there was a history between them, and that today's history lesson was being given at Dan's expense.

The waitress was young, too young for the bartender, and too pretty. Dan guessed her age at about eighteen to the bartender's fifty-one. She was thin, almost too thin, with poor posture. The kind of posture that told people, she didn't want to be noticed, or was afraid to be noticed. With the short denim skirt, and T-shirt that revealed her abdomen however, people were going to notice. Guys were going to notice, and that probably angered an overweight, balding bartender.

Dan wondered what their relationship was. They appeared to be in the middle of some sort of lovers spat. *This girl must have some real self-esteem issues, or really hates Daddy,* Dan thought.

"No one gave me a menu." Dan said, with a smile.

Without a word the girl reached over and took a menu off the table next to Dan's and tossed it onto his table.

"I'll give you some more time," Paula said, as she turned and walked away.

"How was that?" the waitress said to the bartender as she walked by him.

Neither of them made eye contact, but stared straight ahead. The man behind the bar just shook his head slowly, doing his best to hide his growing anger. Dan watched, not realizing that he had a huge grin on his face.

"Glad you can laugh," the bartender said.

Dan got up from his table, and walked over to the bar and sat down.

"Daughter?" Dan said, knowing he was probably wrong.

"Wife," the bartender responded bitterly.

"Oh, sorry," Dan said sticking out his hand. "Dan Coast."

The bartender wiped his big oven mitt of a hand on his loud Aloha shirt and shook.

"I'm sorry too, the name's Jimmy P."

"It looks like the honeymoons over." Dan observed.

"You said it, pal. Some women just need a smack upside the head now and then, ya know what I mean?"

"Not really."

"The little bitch throws herself at half the guys that walk through that door."

Weren't bartenders supposed to be the confessor, not the confessee? Dan mused.

His opinion of Jimmy P. changed quickly. He could see in the man's eyes that his "smack upside the head" comment probably wasn't a joke. He had also noticed a large signet ring on Jimmy's right middle finger. A ring that was about the same size as a small cut on the eye of a certain waitress.

Paula exited the kitchen once again and noticed that Dan was gone. She stopped suddenly and looked around the room, spotted him at the bar, and smiled. It was her first smile of the day.

"Playing musical chairs?" she asked.

The tone of her voice was flirtatious. Dan thought nothing of it. He was sure it was an act to infuriate her husband, and it worked.

"See what I mean?" Jimmy said to Dan, lowering his Borgninian eyebrows and glaring at his young wife.

"Just didn't want to take up a whole table just for me," Dan said to Paula.

The waitress gave Dan a head to toe body scan, liked what she saw. "I can sit with you if you like."

"Get back to the kitchen!" Jimmy bawled.

"Hey, I didn't do anything," Dan said, shaking his head and putting his hands in the air.

"Don't worry about it, pal. She'll get hers later. Now, what can I get ya?" Jimmy said. Dan noticed how the bartender's left hand strayed to his right, fingering the gaudy ring there.

"I'll just have the fish sandwich and fries, and another tequila," Dan said, opting out of the flame-mingo broiled steak, tempting as it sounded.

Dan's lunch came quickly. He felt as though he was being rushed, like Jimmy saw him as a threat to his marriage, and wanted him gone. Dan didn't take this too personal; he could tell that Jimmy was an asshole, and probably felt this way about any guy who came through the door. This, along with the worry of what might happen to Paula after his departure, made Dan eat a lot slower than usual. The longer he stayed, the longer it would be until she felt that ring upside her head again. He finished his second drink and ordered another, sipping it slowly. All the while he could hear muffled arguing going on behind the swinging door.

Paula never appeared again throughout lunch. Another waitress took over her tables, and Jimmy waited grudgingly on Dan when he wasn't standing at the other end of the bar with arms crossed, looking pissed.

Upon Dan's arrival, Jimmy appeared to be a happy-go-lucky type of guy; he smiled and seemed friendly, a genuinely nice guy. Dan was fooled, probably the same way Paula was fooled when she first met Jimmy.

Jimmy slowly became scary after their meeting, as the dark drug of jealousy turned Jekyll into Hyde. Dan wasn't scared, but he could imagine how scared an eighteen-year-old wife, and waitress might be.

Dan set up the whole scenario in his head, just the way he always did. She was young, pretty, and shy, taken in by a smooth talking older man. An older man with money, not a lot, but more than she was used to. She had led a sheltered life, not been allowed to date. When she got her chance to get out of the small town she was raised in, she took it. She quickly accepted his proposal of marriage, and things went downhill from there. Now she was accused of things she never did. Slapped around by her husband, the same way she was once slapped around by her father. Now she was trapped with nowhere to go, and too afraid to try and leave.

Dan didn't know if this was the way things really were, but it angered him just the same. But if she wasn't going to ask for help, then he wasn't going to offer it. It was none of his business, and it was time for him to leave. He paid the check that had been laid next to him along with his meal. He got up, looked around. There was no one to exchange the post-dining pleasantries with ... No "hey, see ya later." No, "thanks for coming." Dan turned and walked out.

As Coast walked through the doors and onto the front porch he looked to his right. The geezer was still sitting there.

"How's it going?" Dan asked.

The man tilted his straw hat back, spurted another stream of chaw juice on the ground. "Better for me than for you. Your plans have changed."

"Oh yeah, why's that?" Dan asked, grinning.

"You'll see," the codger said, nodding toward Dan's car.

Dan wondered what the old man meant by that, but didn't question the ramblings of a loafer on a porch, and kept walking toward his car. Nothing seemed unusual.

As he got to his car, however, it became a little clearer. He had a passenger. There was Paula, scrunched down in the passenger seat with a small suit case on her lap, looking up at Dan. Before Dan could respond, he heard yelling behind him. It was Jimmy.

Paula! Paula! You little bitch!" he was shouting. "Where the hell are you? You better get back in here if you know what's good for ya."

Dan looked from Jimmy back down to Paula.

"Please," she said, "get me out of here, please."

Dan opened the door and slid in as Paula hunkered lower in her seat. Dan started the car and hauled ass out of the parking lot as Paula jumped to her knees on the seat, kissed Dan on the cheek, and waved out the back of the car at Jimmy.

"See ya around, you fat piece of shit!" she shouted, as Dan spun the tires, kicking up a shower of dirt and gravel in Jimmy P.'s astonished face.

Chapter Three

"Are we there yet?" Paula asked, opening her eyes and stretching her arms above her head.

The question she asked was just another reminder in a long list that revealed her young age. *What's next?* Dan thought; *I gotta go to the bathroom. I'm hungry. Or maybe: Dad, Billy's hitting me.*

During her nap, Dan had looked over on several occasions. He noticed how much younger she looked while sleeping. How the stress left her face. He also noticed how her short skirt inched its way up her thigh as she slept. *Dirty old man.*

"About forty-five minutes." Dan said.

"How long was I out?"

"About a half hour or so,"

"Thank you for getting me out of there."

"You're welcome."

"So what now?"

"Well, that's up to you. Is there some place you want to go? Home, maybe? Where are you from?" Dan stopped, realizing he was asking questions much faster than she could answer.

"Can I just stay with you?"

"Stay with me?"

"Sure. I can't pay you, or anything, but I can cook … and clean."

Dan shot her a lopsided grin. "So, you want to leave one master for another?"

"*Very* funny. Well, I kind of feel like I owe you."

Dan waved his hand. "You don't owe me anything. You can stay for a few days, until you figure out what you're going to do."

"Thank you, thank you!" Paula said as she threw her arms around Dan and gave him a big kiss on the mouth.

"And there will be none of that while you're staying with me," Dan said turning his head to cut the kiss short.

"You think you're too old for me?" Paula said, giggling, with her arms still around Dan and her lips almost touching his ear.

"No, I don't think I'm too old for you," Dan replied, "I think you're too young for me."

Paula removed her grip on Dan and returned to her seat, still smiling. She reached down and turned on the radio.

"Oh, Jimmy Buffett!" she squealed. "My grandfather used to listen to this."

Grandfather? Jeez, Dan thought. "Swell," he said. "So grampa was a Parrothead."

Paula eyed him dubiously. "A what?"

"You know, a diehard Buffett fan. Like me."

She shook her head. "No. He never went to any concerts or anything like that. Just had a couple of old records."

Old records. Dan pictured the old man playing ancient records made of stone on a phonograph, a pterodactyl's beak pressed against the record.

As the two drove along, they continued to make small talk, mostly about The Keys, music, and movies. Dan didn't ask any of the obvious questions. How old are you? Where are you from? How did you end up married to that asshole? Instead he let her direct the conversation. There would be plenty of time for those questions later. Right now, he figured, she needed a friend, not a parent.

Dan was starting to notice that the further Paula got from Jimmy the more her self-confidence grew, as well as her sense of humor. Her posture straightened, and there was virtually no stress left in her eyes. It was as though Jimmy was losing the tight grip he had around her throat. She was turning into a different woman before his eyes. A confident woman. A beautiful, confident, sexy woman. Dan imagined this was the woman Jimmy had first gotten a hold of. The woman he tried his best to ruin. He didn't; she was still in there.

Chapter Four

Dan and Paula drove past the sign that read, "WELCOME TO KEY WEST, PARADISE USA", Paula whipped out her cell phone and took a picture. She turned the phone around and looked at the picture she had just taken and smiled.

"I feel like I'm on vacation," she said, turning the phone on Dan and snapping another picture.

"You've never been to Key West before?" Dan asked.

"No. Jimmy never took me anywhere after we were married. He got angry if anyone looked at me, and accused me of looking at every guy that walked by. He took me to Orlando once, to Disney World, before we were married. We left early though. He said I was flirting with a guy that was in line in front of us at the Pirates of the Caribbean ride. I kind of was, I guess. I've just always been like that. I don't usually mean anything by it. I'm just friendly to people who are friendly to me."

Paula fiddled with her phone as she continued. "When we went back to the hotel. I tried to apologize to

Jimmy. That was the first time he ever hit me. Nothing too serious, just a quick back hand across the side of my head. It wasn't hard enough to leave a mark or anything."

"They say a girl remembers her first time," Dan said, trying to make light of an uncomfortable situation.

"Ha-ha. It wasn't the first time someone hit me, just the first time Jimmy hit me." Paula suddenly snapped off her seatbelt and drew her knees under herself in the seat as she turned to face Dan. "Ya know how in those Lifetime movies, Dan," she said, her voice growing animated, "when a guy hits his wife for the first time, he comes to her later and apologizes, and promises things will be different, and he swears he'll never do it again?"

"Yeah, I've seen the movies."

"Jimmy never did that, He never said he was sorry. He never said it wouldn't happen again. He always let me know it was my fault, and that I should be sorry for making him hit me. He made it a point of letting me know that the next time would be worse … and it usually was."

Dan had no response. He could see the pain in Paula's eyes, and he felt it too. He wondered what evil could be inside someone that would make them capable of hitting this young girl. This girl that looked no more harmless than a small kitten.

"Put your seatbelt on," he said casually, "I don't want to get a ticket."

Paula obliged, turned back toward the window, and leaned her head out past the protection of the windshield, letting the wind blow through her long, light brown hair. She reached her arms above her head as though she was trying to fly. Her small white tank top lifted slightly to reveal a bruise on the small of her back. Dan shook his head, but said nothing. He wondered, *Was that an accident, or the temporary reminder of a permanent scar?*

He had no way of knowing, but it angered him all the same.

Dan took a right off Roosevelt onto Flagler. As they drove down the street Paula rested her head on the door and watched the houses and the palm trees as they went past them. After a few blocks Dan took a left onto Fourteenth and pulled into a grocery store parking lot. He figured he better get a few things in his fridge and cupboards if he was going to have a house guest for a few days.

"I'm gonna run in here and grab a few things, is there anything you need, or want?" Dan asked.

"Yeah, I need tampons," Paula said, with no expression.

"Um… uh… what do I__?"

"I'm just busting your balls, dude," Paula said, grinning. "I'm fine."

Dan walked into the store; his face was redder than the tomatoes on the ad in the window.

"Hi, Dan, how ya doin?" said a tall woman with short, curly hair, the color of carrot juice, standing behind a cash register.

Tall was an understatement. Sally was about six-foot-two, and her thin frame made her look even taller. She was proud of her height, and always stood with perfect posture to showcase it, even wearing high heels more often than not. Larry, Sally's husband measured out at about five-foot-eight, which made for a lot of jokes about their height difference. They were never offended by the joking, and even made jokes about it themselves. People in town still laughed about the morning Larry drove Sally to work. He walked her in to the grocery store and in front of everyone in the place, grabbed a milk crate, turned it over, climbed up on it, and gave her a big, sloppy kiss good bye. Dan was one of the patrons that morning and busted a gut laughing along with everyone else.

"Wonderful, Sally!" Dan replied, smiling. "How are you today?"

"Good, but not wonderful," Sally said with a smile. "Why's your face all red, someone just tell ya a dirty joke?"

"Yeah, I'll tell ya later."

Dan's response was almost always "wonderful" when someone asked him how his day was going. Sometimes his response was "super" or something to that effect, but almost always "wonderful." Anyone who knew Dan knew to expect this reply. Dan didn't know exactly when he started using that line, or even why, but he knew people expected it, and he always delivered. He thought it was amusing how some people smiled at his response. Some thought he was being sarcastic, and others seemed angry that he was having a better day than them.

Coast walked up and down the aisles with his grocery cart, the front wheel wobbling, and squeaking as he went along. He breezed by the canned goods. *Ate enough of that shit when I was a kid*. He breezed by the meats, the fruits, and the vegetables. He breezed by various products in small cardboard boxes, marked "new" and "improved" and "better tasting."

When Dan got to the register there was only five items in his cart: milk, Pop-Tarts, the kind with no frosting, the best kind, two limes, and Frosted Flakes. Sally leaned over the counter, and peered critically into his cart.

"Are you gonna need help getting all that stuff to your car, Dan?" she asked.

Dan put the items on the counter. Sally rang them up.

"I don't know what to get. What does a young girl eat?" Dan asked.

"How young?" Sally replied, cocking an eyebrow as she held up the Pop Tarts.

"She's just a friend."

"Uh-huh. Now I know why you was blushing. That'll be twenty-seven dollars and thirteen cents."

Dan paid Sally in cash and exited the store. Walking back across the parking lot he could see Paula leaning against the car. She was watching a group of young men in a skate board park across the street. They would skate down one side of the plywood ramp and up the other. Some would spin in the air holding their skate boards. Inevitably some poor sap would take a nasty fall, shake off his hurts and the taunts of his friends, and do it all over again. One boy had a video camera and filmed his friends as they defied gravity and good sense. Dan knew they were probably doing tricks that had cool names, but he didn't know what they were. Paula probably did, though, another nail in the generation gap coffin.

"They look like they're having fun." Paula said gleefully.

"They wear girl's pants." Dan snorted, tossing the groceries into the car.

Chapter Five

The Porsche pulled into the driveway of the white, one-story bungalow with green shutters, at 632 Beach View Street.

Dan and Paula climbed out of the Porsche, and walked toward the house.

"Did someone run into your tree?" Paula said, noticing the blue gouge on the side of the palm tree in Dan's front yard.

"Yeah, somebody," Dan said, as he led Paula up the steps and onto the porch.

When Dan got to his front door, he bent down, folded back the welcome mat that read THE COAST'S. He picked up the not-so-secret key, wiped off the dirt, unlocked the door and entered.

Paula asked, "Don't you worry about robbers?"

Dan grunted, "I'm hoping they worry about me."

Once inside, Paula scampered from room to room like a new puppy brought home for the first time. Dan hoped she was housebroken.

"How do you get upstairs?" Paula asked.

Ask a stupid question... "There is no upstairs that's the beauty of a one-story house."

"There's only one bathroom."

"I only *need* one bathroom."

"What about me?"

"We'll have to share a bathroom, your majesty. Is that okay?"

"I guess," Paula replied, disgustedly.

"Why, how many bathrooms are you used to?"

"We have five in our house."

"*Five?* You mean to tell me you have five bathrooms over that pissant bar and grill?"

"I don't live over the bar and grill," Paula said, matter-of-factly, "I live in a *house*. Jimmy and I have a huge house. Six bedrooms and five bathrooms. We even have our own little movie theater. We have a pool and a hot tub too."

"So why would a husband and wife who live in a *giant* mansion wait tables and tend bar in a roadside greasy spoon?"

"We were just there for the day, smartass. Jimmy likes to drive around to all his places about once a month, just to make sure everything is running smooth, and no one is ripping him off. While we're there he works the bar and he always makes me work too."

"Ripping him off?" Dan asked. "*All* of his places?"

"Yeah, *all* of his places. Jimmy owns a few bars and restaurants around the state. He keeps a real good watch on all his property and all his employees too. Jimmy treats his employees pretty good, loans them money, buys them gifts, but if he finds out someone is screwing him, he gets pretty mean."

"Yeah. He struck me as a real sonofabitch underneath that affable bear exterior."

Paula nodded. "Yeah. I remember this one time we went up to Orlando to this little bar he owns. The manager had told Jimmy that one of the bartenders was caught on camera stealing money out of the cash register. Jimmy said he would handle it. When we got there Jimmy pulled into an alley behind the bar and went in through the back door. I waited in the car."

"A few minutes later he came walking out with this kid, probably about twenty-five years old or so. Jimmy made the kid put his hand on the hood of the car. Then he took a hammer out of the inside pocket of his jacket and smashed the kids hand. He hit that kids hand probably three or four times. The kid was crying, and saying he was sorry. Jimmy let go of the kid's hand and he fell down on his knees. He was grabbing Jimmy's shirt with his good hand begging him not to kill him. Jimmy just looked at him and said," Paula did her best Tony Soprano impression. 'That's what happens after strike one, you don't want there to be no strike two.'

"Then he told the kid that the damage to the hood of the car would be deducted from his pay. He told the kid to take a couple days off, but make sure he was back to work on Monday. We even gave the kid a ride home. He was sobbing in the back seat the whole way. He just kept saying, 'I'm sorry, Jimmy, I'm sorry!' with his hand wrapped in a towel. The kid was hurt bad but both of us knew better than to suggest Jimmy should take him to the emergency room. I guess he saw a doctor after he got home. At least I hope so. But I know one thing, he didn't tell no doctor what really happened to his hand."

Dan stood motionless, staring at Paula, his head lowered, trying to pick out something to say out of the endless list going through his head. *Who is this guy*? he thought.

"I bet driving away with his wife is probably a strike one," was the thing Dan settled on saying first.

"Probably," Paula said, shaking her head.

"By the way, what does the P stand for in Jimmy P.?" Dan asked.

"Pantucco."

"Big Jimmy Pantucco? Your husband is *Big Jimmy Pantucco*?" Dan asked, his voice cracking like Peter Brady singing, "It's a Sunshine Day."

"Yeah, that's what his friends call him," Paula said. "Big Jimmy."

"Jesus Christ!" Dan said, putting his hands over his face. "What the fuck did I do?"

"You rescued me."

"But I may have killed myself doing it."

Paula walked over to the table and looked in the grocery bag.

"Pop-Tarts and cereal? I hope that's not dinner." Paula said, making a face.

"Let me guess, five bathrooms *and* you've never eaten Pop-Tarts for supper."

"Not since I was a kid."

"And now that you're all grown up?" Dan asked sarcastically.

"I like big people food." Paula smiled. "I stopped ordering off the children's menu years ago."

"I need a drink." Dan said walking toward the bar.

"Me too, but first a shower. Which bedroom is mine?"

"End of the hall on the left."

Paula had her shirt unbuttoned by the time she got to the bedroom door, and removed her bra as she disappeared into the room, revealing nothing. *Perfect timing*, Dan thought as he watched her walk out of sight, *little tease*.

Dan finished making his drink and walked out the kitchen door, down the stairs, and along the gravel path to the Adirondack chairs by the fire pit. He sat down put up his feet, and leaned his head back. He glanced around. As usual Buddy was AWOL. *Man's best friend, my ass.*

"I just wanted something to eat," He said aloud, "And where's that goddamn dog?"

Chapter Six

"Hey, sleepy head," Paula whispered in Dan's ear, startling him.

Dan jumped, spilling the water in his glass left from the ice. He looked at his wrist, an old habit left over from the days when time mattered. The days when he wore the gold watch his wife had bought him for Christmas. Dan took off the wrist watch shortly after arriving in Paradise USA and never put it on again. It now lays in an old ash tray on the night stand next to his bed. A painful reminder of a wife that left too soon.

"Don't sneak up on me like that." Dan groused.

"Sorry," Paula said, "you were talking in your sleep. It looked like you were having a nightmare."

She walked over to the other Adirondack chair and sat down, leaning back, and crossing her legs to reveal most of her thigh. She was wearing a robe she had found hanging on the back of the bathroom door. The robe was pink, and short, and tied at the waist. She left a small opening in the front to showcase the area between what she regarded as her size perfect breasts. Big Jimmy held the same opinion. So did Dan. On Dan's patented bikini fruit comparison chart, her tits scored a honeydew melon rating. Honeydews that were Grade A, USDA Inspected, Number One Pure Choice. *Ripe and natural,* Dan thought.

Paula had kept her eyes locked on Dan's through the whole seating process to see where he looked, what he noticed, and how he reacted. Dan kept his eyes locked on hers, trying to beat her at her own game. Dan hated it when women played games, and now this girl had pulled him into hers. She grinned, knowing it was killing Dan not to look.

Paula had made herself a drink. From the dark color Dan knew it was Scotch, straight up, and judging from her lack of expression when she swallowed, it wasn't the first time she had drank neat Scotch.

"I had to make my own drink," Paula said, complainingly.

"Are you old enough for that?" Dan asked.

"Yes. I am... and who's Alex?"

The question caught Dan off guard. He looked almost frightened, and Paula could see it in his face.

"You mentioned him in your sleep."

"She wasn't a he. She was my wife."

"Divorced?"

"No. She was killed in a car accident."

"I'm sorry."

"Don't be. Shit happens..."

"... and some days it's piled a little higher than others right?" Paula added.

"How old are you, anyway," Dan asked, steering the conversation in a different direction.

"Twenty-four," she replied, her answer sounding like a coquettish invitation.

Dan was doubtful. Paula looked to be around eighteen or nineteen. He knew she was probably older than that, but would never have guessed she was much over twenty. Sitting across from him now, with wet straight hair and no makeup, she sure didn't look twenty-four. Not that her age mattered, she was still a mobster's wife. Driving away with her was bad enough. Sleeping with her would be certain death.

"How old is Jimmy?" Dan asked.

"Fifty-two."

"How long have you been married?"

"A little over three years. Would you like me to make you another drink Dan?" Paula asked, changing the subject.

"Sure. Tequila, Seven, and lime," Dan answered, holding out his glass.

"Are you hungry, Dan? I could fix you a Pop-Tart, or some Frosted Flakes," Paula said as she walked back up the gravel path toward the back door.

"Either one is fine."

Dan watched as she walked away. Paula knew he was watching, and Dan knew she knew, but he didn't care. For once Paula wasn't staring at him, waiting for a reaction, and he was going to take advantage of it. He felt a little guilty, however, watching another woman's ass wiggle up his pathway in Candi's robe. He felt even more guilty thinking how much better Paula looked in it than Candi had. At least now he knew Paula was twenty-four so some of the dirty old man guilt he had been carrying around had subsided.

Dan figured Candi probably didn't want the robe back anyway, or else she would have taken it with her last month when she came down from Miami and picked up her other things.

The breakup was for the most part, uneventful. There was no yelling, no fighting, and no arguing of any kind. There was just a long discussion about long distance relationships, and Dan's extra baggage. There was talk of Dan's drinking, and his immaturity. Looking back, Dan remembered most of the conversation being about his short comings. There was mention of still being friends, and calling if you're in town. Dan knew he would never call, and figured she probably wouldn't either.

After Candi went back to Miami, Dan had noticed that she left the robe hanging on the bathroom door, and a photograph of the two of them on the night stand on her side of the bed. He figured she had left them as a reminder, a way of saying look at what you were too stupid to hold on to. Dan looked at the photograph for a few days, and then stuck it in a duffle bag under some floor boards, beneath a loose piece of carpet in his closet, along with other mementos from that chapter in his life. He put the floor boards back in place and folded the rug back, and that chapter was closed.

He had forgotten about the robe until now, but in the future, it wouldn't be Candi he thought about when he saw the robe. So it could stay above the floor boards.

Paula returned shortly with a fresh drink for Dan, and as a joke, a Pop-Tart on a plate, with a knife, fork, and a folded paper towel lying alongside.

"Here you go, master," she said, bowing low before handing Dan the glass and plate.

"Okay, okay, I can take a hint. Let me take a shower and get dressed. We'll go grab something to eat," Dan said, climbing out of his chair.

"Oh, I should have waited, we could have taken one together and saved some water," Paula said with her usual devilish grin.

Dan shook his head as he walked up the gravel pathway to the back door.

Chapter Seven

Dan reached down and turned the hot and cold handles of his shower to the off position, turned and slid back the shower curtain to see Paula standing at the mirror applying her makeup. She was dressed. White shorts, with the bottoms frayed to give that cut offs look. She had on a tan T-shirt with a picture of a life guard tower running down the left side, and white sneakers with no socks. Her hair was still wet, pulled back tightly into a pony tail. Her legs were tan and thin, and showed every muscle when she leaned forward to apply the war paint. It caught Dan off guard to see her standing there, her clothed, him naked.

"Hey there, big fella," Paula said her eyes never leaving the mirror.

Dan quickly grabbed a towel off the towel bar and wrapped it around his waist.

"Big fella?"

She giggled. "I peeked behind the curtain when I came in."

"Listen, Paula, we're going to have to have some ground rules if you're going to stay here. For example, no peeking behind curtains."

Paula's brow furrowed. "Then how will I see out of the windows?"

Chrissy Snow? Dan thought, *or is she busting my balls again?*

"*Shower* curtains. No peeking behind *shower* curtains." Dan said, raising his voice, as he got out of the shower.

As Dan side stepped behind Paula, he glanced in the mirror. He could see she was grinning big and trying not to burst into laughter. She was getting great joy out of his anger and discomfort. Dan was not the type of guy to get easily agitated, or thrown off his game by a female. He was usually the one doing the agitating. But there was something about this girl. She could easily get under his skin, and she enjoyed being there.

As he passed behind her, she stuck out her back side to cause him to brush up against her. Dan rolled his eyes.

"Oooh," Paula purred. "Hell-*o*, big fella!"

If I was ten years younger, he thought, *I'd show her*

"Big fella"all right. Ah who am I kidding? If I was fifteen *years younger, maybe.*

He walked into his bed room, closed the door, removed his towel, and threw it on the bed. He looked back at the doorknob, walked over and locked it.

"Just to be on the safe side…"

Chapter Eight

Dan turned left onto Charles Lake Road. To the right, off into the distance, Paula could see the ocean. She pulled out her cell phone and snapped a few more pictures, turned her phone, looked at the pictures and smiled. *Instant gratification,* Dan thought.

He remembered when you waited a week and a half to see what the picture looked like, and when it came you could hold it in your hand. It was three and a half inches by five inches. The photo had color, it had substance, it had meaning. You would hold the picture and remember where you were, and when you took it.

Now you take a picture, and the first words out of everyone's mouth is, "let me see, let me see it!" and if they had their eyes closed or they were making a stupid face, delete. Photographs just didn't seem to have the same meaning anymore.

Why I remember when I was a kid, Dan thought. *Holy Christ I'm my father.*

Rodney Riesel

"How far is Duvall Street from here?" Paula asked, interrupting Dan's stroll down memory lane.

"Five or six blocks. Why?"

"I saw something about it on the Travel Channel awhile back. Looks like a fun place. Maybe you could take me tonight."

"Maybe tomorrow night, I have to get up early tomorrow morning. I'm going out fishing with a friend of mine."

"Can I go?" Paula asked, excited.

"No."

"Why not?"

"Because I said so. You're not down here on vacation, and I'm not your tour guide. You're going to spend tomorrow figuring out what you're going to do next."

"Yes, sir!" Paula said with her usual grin, and saluted.

She leaned over in her seat, laying her head against Dan's shoulder. Holding her phone out at arm's length, and smiling, she took a picture of the two of them.

"Say cheese," She said.

Dan didn't say cheese, nor did he smile. He couldn't help wondering how much trouble he was already in, and how much more she was going to cause for him, and did he have his eyes closed for the picture, or was he making a stupid face. *Let me see, let me see it*, he thought.

Dan turned into Red's parking lot and backed into the only space that didn't have discarded car litter or broken glass in it.

"Fancy place," Paula sneered sarcastically. "You really know how to show your date a good time. Are you sure you don't want to try a fancier place like Mc Donald's or Taco Bell?"

"You're not my date, and I doubt you're paying. Besides, we don't have a Taco Bell, and the Mc Donald's is all the way on the other side of the island."

"Wow. With sweet talk like that, you just might get lucky tonight."

Dan got out and started walking toward the bar. Paula climbed over the broken passenger door, and ran to catch up with him. As they walked together she reached over to hold his hand.

"Knock that off!" Dan said, pushing her hand away.

"Or what?" Paula grinned. "Are you going to spank me when we get home?"

Dan snorted. "You'd like that, wouldn't you?" *And so would I.*

Red's was Dan's favorite place to eat on the island, and Red was Dan's closest friend on the island. Red's Tiki Bar and Grill was just what the name described. It was wooden planks. It was bamboo. All over the interior walls there was surfing, sailing, and fishing memorabilia. Over the bamboo-lined bar there was a thatched roof, and hanging from the eaves of the thatched roof were a string of small light-up parrots that came in four colors; green, red, yellow, and blue. There was even a totem pole in one corner of the bar. The dining area consisted of six or seven square tables with four chairs at each one. The bar had nine, orange vinyl bar stools, the type that swiveled, but with no arm rests. The jukebox was filled with Buffett, Zac Brown, Bob Marley, Kenny Chesney, and a few other artists that reminded you that you were in Paradise USA.

Dan headed toward the bar and Paula went to a table. Dan saw her out of the corner of his eye and redirected himself toward the same table. They reached the table at the same time. Dan sat, and Paula waited beside her chair, staring at Dan. Red walked up behind Paula and pulled out her chair. She sat.

"Well, at least someone knows how to treat a lady," Paula said.

"And you are …?" Red asked as he also sat down in the chair beside Paula.

"… too young for you," Dan cut in.

"I'm Paula. Dan and I live together," Paula said, holding out her hand.

Red took her hand, and with a great big smile, said, "I'm Red, it's a pleasure to meet you."

"It's a pleasure to meet you as well," Paula said, batting her eye lashes at Red.

"And what can I get you to drink, sweetheart?" Red asked.

"Vodka and cranberry would be nice."

Red winked and said, "One vodka and cranberry coming right up."

"And maybe a tequila, Seven, and lime for me?" Dan asked, shaking his head at Red's momentary lapse into puppy love.

"Sure thing, pal," Red said, never taking his eyes off of Paula.

"Can I have my hand back now, Red? I may need it to eat with," Paula said.

Red quickly let go of Paula's hand and instantly remembered where he was. He walked away from the table and to the bar to fix the drinks. As he walked, his lips moved, and he grinned to himself. It was obvious he was recounting his exchange with Paula, and trying to come up with the next witty line to make the young girl smile. Red didn't seem to realize that it didn't matter what he said next, Paula was going to laugh anyway.

Paula wasn't the type of girl that was made happy by other people. She was the type that made others happy just to get what she wanted. It was becoming more and more evident to Dan that Paula wasn't the sweet, young, innocent girl she had seemed to be in the beginning. She could make herself appear to be helpless, and in need of a knight in shining armor, but Dan was no longer buying it. He was starting to see how Paula and her sarcasm, and her smart mouth, could get her into a lot of trouble with a violent man like Jimmy P. Men like Jimmy don't want their women talking back, or acting in a way that they would call disrespectful. Even though Dan could see the reason for the abuse, he also knew there was no real excuse for it, and if Paula needed his help and a place to stay for a while, she could have it.

Red returned from the bar with the drinks and sat them on the table. He made a few more jokes, and flirted a little, making a slight ass out of himself as usual. Paula laughed at every joke and looked at Red with those big brown eyes, batting her lashes like he was the most important man in the room. Red bought it hook, line, and sinker and felt like he was the most important man in the room, as well as the funniest, smartest, and best looking.

"Are you two just here for drinks, or will you be joining us for dinner?" Red asked.

"We're here for dinner, Red," Paula replied. "All Dan has at his house is Pop-Tarts and Corn Flakes."

Dan glared at her. "They're not Corn Flakes, they're Frosted Flakes."

"Would you like to hear tonight's specials?" Red asked.

"We sure would," Paula said.

Red, squinting his eyes, rambled off the specials as he read them from a chalk board across the room next to the door. "We have a coconut grouper served with a crispy potato cake and vegetables and a Key lime mustard sauce. We have a steamed Maine lobster served with corn on the cob and whole baby red potatoes. And we also have fish and chips with coleslaw and French fries." When he had finished he gave them each a menu and disappeared through a door next to the bar and into the kitchen.

After a few moments Red returned and took their orders, along with an order for himself, so as not to miss an opportunity to sit and have dinner with the young girl who had placed him under her spell for the evening. After taking the orders he again retreated into the kitchen.

"Boy, you sure have an effect on men, don't you?" Dan said to Paula, as Red let the kitchen door close behind him.

Not only did Dan notice the effect she had on Red, but also how almost every guy in the place was trying to sneak a quick look at her. One man sitting alone stared until noticed by Paula; he smiled and gave a little nod. A man sitting with his wife kept looking over, trying not to get caught looking. One man's wife did notice, and was giving Paula the evil eye. A young man at the bar was jabbing his buddy in the ribs with his elbow and pointing at Paula with his head to get the other man to notice her. There was even a young boy of about four years old sitting with his family. He stood backwards in the booth trying to get Paula's attention. When he did, he waved and smiled. She waved back, and he quickly turned around and sat back down embarrassed. There seemed to be no age limit for the men Paula could enchant.

"Yeah, that's what my daddy used to say. He would say, 'Paula, you're like a bitch in heat, and those boys are like rabid dogs trying to get at ya. It's like they lose all control of themselves when they get around ya.' I guess the biggest problem was that Daddy couldn't keep control of himself either. He kept most of the boys away, but he couldn't keep himself away."

Dan sipped his drink. "Your father?"

"Yeah, well .... he wasn't my real father. My real father died before I was born. Fell out of a boat in the swamp, gators got him. Howard is my step dad. He raised me. He should have acted more like a father. I think he would get jealous when other boys would come around. He tried to say he was protecting me, but I could see the way he looked at me. When I was fifteen years old Howie, that's my stepfather's name, caught me out in the wood shed with one of the local boys. We had put a blanket down, Billy lit some candles. He was trying to make it romantic, I guess. He wanted to make me feel special. I told him it was my first time."

"I'm guessing it wasn't," Dan said.

"It wasn't even my first time with someone named Billy," Paula said. She had a faraway look in her eyes as she recalled the story. "I just like making a guy feel special, and that usually makes a guy want to make me feel special."

"Yeah, I've noticed you're pretty good at that," Dan agreed, nodding his head toward Red.

"Oh, he's cute, and look how good it makes him feel. There's no harm in making someone feel good, is there?"

"No, but the problem starts when the guy finally realizes he's *not* special, and then he feels like you've made an ass out of him. I'm guessing that's what happened with your stepfather?"

"That's what happened, all right. He came home half in the bag, caught the two of us in that shed, and he beat the hell outta Billy. He drug me in the house by the hair, calling me a little tease, and a no-good whore," Paula lowered her voice, the sarcastic smile had left her face. "He threw me on the living room floor. He finally got what he wanted that night, whether I wanted it or not. I tried to fight him off. I tried to call out for my mother, but he had his hand over my mouth. Finally I just figured the sooner I gave in, the sooner it would be over. I just turned my head and laid there on the living room floor, all still like, and let him finish. My mother was sound asleep upstairs. She never heard a thing, or maybe she did, who knows."

"Did you ever tell your mother?"

"No. Howard said if I ever told anyone, he would kill me, my brother, and my mother, and I believed him. The next morning I packed a few things, took a hundred and thirty five bucks out of Howard's dresser drawer, and left. I've never been back."

"Where did you go?"

"I took a bus to Miami. I had an aunt that lived there. I stayed with her for a while, but that didn't work out. Her boyfriend was no better than Howard. Then I moved in with a couple of girls I had met at the beach. I got a job washing dishes in a small diner. Even got my GED. When I turned eighteen I got a job serving drinks in a little strip joint. Eventually I started dancing a little, maybe one or two nights a week, when a girl didn't show up or something. That's where I met Jimmy. He owned the place. We dated for a few weeks and he asked me to marry him, so I did ... and that's the story of my life."

Dan reared back in his seat and sighed. Not his usual world-weary sigh, but a sympathetic one. "That's some story."

"Yeah, Lifetime movie, right?"

As Paula finished up her story, Cindy, Red's bartender came through the front door. She was red faced, and it was obvious she had been crying. Her puffy eyes betrayed little sleep. Her hair was tied back in a sloppy ponytail. She was wearing denim shorts and a wrinkled white T-shirt. She walked behind the bar without a word to anyone, and put on her apron. She turned on the water and filled the sink under the bar, wet a bar towel and started wiping down the bar. As she wiped the bar with her left hand, the index finger of her right hand kept going to each eye to wipe away the continuous buildup of tears. Every few minutes she made a sobbing sound as though she was trying to catch her breath, like a small child who had been crying in their crib for hours.

"I wonder what it is this time?" Red asked, as he brought the three plates to the table and sat down.

"What do you mean, this time," Dan asked, cutting into his steak.

"Her and Derrick have been getting into it pretty good the last few days while you were away. Fighting constantly. He calls here every night to make sure she's really here working."

"Where else would she be?" Paula asked.

"Well one night, the first of last week," Red said, turning toward Paula, who was obviously more interested in his story than her food, "she told Derrick she had to work, but instead she went to meet an old boyfriend for dinner. Derrick called here from work to talk to her. Jock, that's my cook, told him she wasn't working that night. Well from what Phil told me, that's Derrick's boss over at Island Adventures, Derrick went crazy, throwing things. Shit, he broke a computer, broke the phone. This all happened in front of a couple of customers. I guess he had been suspicious for a few days and as far as he was concerned this was all the proof he needed that she was cheating on him."

"*Was* she cheating on him?" Paula asked, wide eyed.

"I guess not. According to her, the old boyfriend said he just wanted to talk to her about some paper work he had come across, and he needed her signature on a few things. I guess the two of them came down here on spring break a few years ago with friends. At the time the two of them were engaged and had already filed for their marriage license, had a couple joint accounts, things like that. Now I guess he's getting married and needs to tie up some loose ends. I guess they just had dinner and she signed a few papers and that was it. She tried to explain it to Derrick, but he wouldn't believe her."

"That's too bad, poor girl." Paula frowned. "Maybe I should talk to her."

"Yeah, maybe you should," Dan grunted. "Over there where I can't hear it. Christ, it's like a story line from Days of Our Lives, and listening to you two gossips tell it is giving me a headache."

Paula got up and walked slowly and cautiously toward the bar where Cindy was still doing more tasks than needed, just to keep her mind off her stormy love life.

"Hi, Cindy, can I get three more drinks?" Paula asked cheerily.

"Yes, what can I …," Cindy said, breaking down in the middle of her sentence.

She put her hands over her face and began to sob. Paula went around behind the bar and put her hand on Cindy's back."

"I'm sorry." Cindy whimpered.

"That's okay, let it out, we've all been there." Paula consoled her. "Do you want to talk about it? I know you don't know me, but sometimes it helps to talk about it."

Cindy shook her head yes. She took off the apron, laid it on the bar, and the two young women walked together out the front door. Dan watched through the window as they walked across the parking lot to a grassy area where there were two red picnic tables. Each picnic table had an umbrella, white and yellow, with the words Corona Extra written across them. The two girls sat at one of the tables opposite each other.

Introductions out of the way, Paula asked, "So, what's wrong?"

Cindy flung up her arms helplessly. "Where should I start? What's *not* wrong?"

"Well, Red told us about the boyfriend coming down to see you. He told us about dinner, signing papers, and he told us about the fight. Why don't you start from there?"

"Maybe we should just have Red come out and sit with us and he can finish the story."

"That's funny," Paula said, as both girls laughed.

"There's more to the story." Cindy said, growing serious.

Paula smiled knowingly. "There always is. Tell me about it."

"A couple of weeks ago I got a call from Mark, that's my ex," Cindy began. "He wanted to come down to talk to me about something, I told him I didn't want him to come down. He kept calling. He finally told me he was getting married, and he needed me to sign some papers. I agreed to meet him. When he got here he called me to have me meet him for dinner. Come to find out, he was staying at my parent's house; they have a house here on the island. I went to the house. We had dinner delivered, had a few drinks, talked about old times, laughed. One thing led to another and we slept together.

"Come to find out, there were no papers to sign. He wasn't getting married. He came down here to try and get me back. He wanted me to come back home with him. I got angry and left. I didn't get home till two in the morning. Derrick was out of his mind, yelling throwing things. I didn't tell him what happened, but he could tell."

"Did he hit you?"

Cindy shook her head emphatically. "No! He never has, and he never would."

"What are you going to do? Are you staying with Derrick, or going back with Mark?"

"I'm staying here. I love it here, and I love Derrick. We just have to work through this."

"Where's Derrick now?"

"He's still at our apartment. I told him I need some space, time to think things over. I've stayed at Dan's the last couple of nights. He always tells me when he's going away so I can go over and feed Buddy and bring in the mail for him. I knew he wouldn't mind if I stayed there, but I'll probably head home after work now that he's home."

"Why didn't you just stay at your parent's house?"

"Mark's still there. He said he was going to stay on the island a few more days, try to change my mind. I didn't think it would be a good idea for me to stay there with him."

"I guess not," Paula agreed.

The two girls talked for a little while longer, getting to know each other a little better. Paula told Cindy a little about her marital situation. She told Cindy the story of how Dan had come into a local bar just to get something to eat and ended up saving a poor, abused young woman. They cried a little, laughed a little and eventually walked back across the parking lot toward the bar and grill, hand in hand, as though they had been friends for years.

"Let's head back into the bar and ask Red if there is anything I left out of my story," Cindy said, as they shared a laugh.

The girls entered the bar together giggling like school girls. Dan and Red were still at their table, just finishing up the second drink that they had had to make for themselves in the absence of a bartender.

"All better ladies?" Dan asked, as the girls walked through the doors.

"All better sweetheart. I'm glad you and I don't have these problems," Paula said to Dan with her usual grin.

"There *is* no us, sweetheart," Dan corrected her. "and ya know, between the two of you ladies there's about ten years of bartending experience. Do you think I could get one more for the road? I'd like to get to bed at a decent hour, since I have a long day of fishing ahead of me."

Paula went behind the bar and made a drink for Dan and Red, and a drink for Cindy and herself as well. She brought them to the table on a tray. Red, not taking his eyes off Paula, noticed she was very efficient in her bartending skills.

"We could use one more bartender around here if you're interested, Paula," Red said, hopefully.

"I don't think so, Red. Dan and I like living a life of leisure." She winked at Dan. "Thanks anyway."

Paula headed toward the jukebox. Halfway across the floor she turned, walked back toward Dan. With her hand out in front of her she rubbed her thumb and fingers together. Dan didn't flinch, but Red reached quickly for his wallet. Pulling it from his back pocket he separated the Velcro with a rip and opened the blue nylon tri-fold. Red pulled a five dollar bill from the wallet and handed it to Paula who gave him a quick kiss on the forehead as a reward, spun around and made her way back toward the jukebox, a gorgeous, surprisingly well-maintained 1950s-era Seeburg Select-O-Matic that was lit up like a carnival.

Dan glared at Red. "Good boy."

"What?" Red feigned indignation. "She just wants to play the frickin' *jutebox.*"

Nineteen eighty four called, they want their wallet back," Dan deadpanned. "And it's *jukebox* not *jutebox*.

"What's wrong with my wallet? And sorry if I don't pronounce every word correctly, you know I can't hear out of my left ear."

"What?"

"What?"

"Huh?"

"You're a prick."

"You're the first person to ever call me that."

Chapter Nine

The blue, (with spots of gray primer) 2003 Porsche 911 Carrera convertible pulled into Dan's driveway a little after midnight. It was much later than Dan had wanted to get home. Dan was too drunk to drive, and Paula, being just a little drunker than Dan decided she should be the designated driver for the evening. Dan didn't argue.

She skidded to a stop and the car's front bumper came to rest on top of the bottom step of the front porch with a dull thud. Dan's head hit the visor. Both drunks looked at each other in surprise, and burst into laughter. At this point in the evening, everything was funny.

"I think you dented my beautiful car," Dan laughed.

"I don't think anyone's going to notice," Paula returned.

"Hey, I love this car. It's German engineering at its finest. Porsche. There is no substitute," Dan replied in his best Sgt. Shultz.

"You would think with your money, you would buy something a little nicer."

"Oh, and what do you drive, little miss wealthy Mafia wife?" Dan asked, his speech slightly slurred. "A limo, I suppose."

"No, I drive a 2011 Volkswagen Bug. It's pink. Jimmy bought it for me just before we came down here. A prize for being able to take a punch I guess."

"Wow! A *brand new* Bug. German engineering at its *second* finest. Volkswagen, there is a substitute" Dan said sarcastically, using his German accent once again.

"Well, not new exactly, but new to me. We walked out of the house together and it was sitting in the driveway with a big red bow on top. He threw me the keys and said, "Here, baby, you drive. Daddy bought you a new car.""

"Daddy?" Dan asked.

"Jimmy liked it when I called him Daddy. Kinda weird, huh?"

"Kinda weird," Dan replied.

"I always thought so too. Anyway, I started it up. The dash board lights up, showing 15,700 miles. I turned to Jimmy and said, 'New car huh? What happened to the last owner?' He just looked at me, grinned, and said, 'If the last owner ever learns to drive again, it'll be in one of those special vans for gimps.' Then he lets out this big laugh, like he was so proud of himself."

"…And what do you mean 'with all my money'?" Dan asked, belatedly following up Paula's earlier remark.

Paula shrugged. "Oh, Cindy let it slip that you had won the lottery or something, and that you were loaded."

"She did, did she?"

"Are you?"

"Am I what?"

"Are you loaded?"

Dan simply replied, "No man is rich enough to buy back his past."

"Oscar Wilde," Paula put in.

"Um … yeah," Dan responded, surprised.

"I'm not stupid."

"*Apparently not*, thought Dan, but responded with, "I never said you were."

Forgetting the car door didn't open, Dan gave the handle a tug and rolled his eyes.

Paula grinned. "Trapped."

"Not hardly."

Dan grabbed the top of the windshield with both hands and hoisted himself up out of his seat. He climbed over the windshield and on to the hood of the car. He turned and held out his hand to Paula. She played along, took his hand and followed suit. She walked across the hood slowly with her arms outstretched like a high wire walker.

"Watch out for the sharks," Paula whispered.

"What?" Dan asked.

"It … was just a game me and my brother played when we were kids. We would walk around the living room on the furniture, and pretend the floor was the ocean. We would jump from the couch to the chair, to the ottoman. If one of us fell, we would pretend sharks were eating us."

Dan turned and grabbed a hold of Paula's shoulders and pretended to push her off the car, into the pretend shark-infested ocean below. "Watch out for sharks." He pulled her back toward him. She stared up into his eyes, their faces inches apart.

"That's the second time you saved my life today," Paula said quite somberly.

Dan jumped from the car to the porch steps, turned and held out his hand saying, "Miss." Paula took it and also jumped to the porch.

"Thank you, gallant sir."

As they walked into the house Paula headed down the hallway to the bathroom, and Dan made the two of them another drink. Scotch on the rocks for Paula and tequila and Seven for himself. He remembered the limes he had bought earlier, but it was late and he was too lazy to slice one.

Dan sat in his chair watching TV, the volume turned down low, sipping his drink. He had removed his flip-flops and was rubbing his feet back and forth on the cool oak floor. An ancient Barnaby Jones rerun he had seen a thousand times flickered before him.

Paula slowly walked from the hall into the living room. Her hair was down now. She was wearing only her T-shirt. She reached over and flipped off the wall switch. The room was now lighted only by the TV. She walked slowly toward Dan. As she walked in front of the light of the TV, Dan could see her perfect shape through the thin cotton. She came closer, crossing her arms in front of her and grabbing the bottom of the T-shirt, she pulled it off over her head. She straddled Dan, sitting on his lap, facing him. She leaned in, slowly kissed his chin, his cheek, the bridge of his nose. She put her lips to his, but not kissing. She slid her lips across his and went to his neck, and then back to his lips. Dan could hold out no longer. He grabbed the back of her head and pulled her in toward him. As they kissed Dan's hands explored every inch of her body. Paula unbuttoned Dan's shirt and opened it. His chest was moist with small beads of sweat. Paula pushed her chest hard against his and let out a small moan as she kissed his neck.

There was a buzzing, a vibrating, and another small light illuminated the room. It was Paula's phone. She pushed back from Dan, sat quietly, and stared at him blank-faced; he didn't move or say a word. The phone vibrated again. Her eyes went to the phone on the end table beside them, and then back to Dan. It vibrated a third time. She reached for the phone, pressed a button, and put it up to her ear.

"Hello?" she said quietly, her voice shaking.

She sat perfectly still. Dan could hear an inaudible voice at the other end of Paula's phone.

"It's for you," Paula said, holding the phone out to Dan.

There was no expression on Dan's face. He was not puzzled. He was not surprised. This was a call he was expecting. He didn't know where or when the call might come, but he knew who would be making it. He took the phone from Paula.

"Yes?" Dan said into the cell phone, his voice lower than usual.

"Dan Coast," came the voice from the other end, "you're an easy man to track down. Dan Coast, lottery winner, born in upstate New York, thirty-nine years old, self-employed contractor, wife killed by the family dog. Tragic story."

Dan recognized the voice immediately; the swaggering, Robert De Niroish kind of voice you could imagine saying "fugettaboutit." He knew it was Jimmy. The voice was the same, but had taken on a different tone since their earlier conversation. Jimmy spoke slowly, annunciating each word. His voice was low and calm. Dan imagined that this was the last voice a lot of unfortunate bastards heard right before the pop of a gunshot to the back of the head. Dan was a little nervous, too, but he wasn't about to show it. The distance between two phones can embolden a man as well as three shots of tequila. Dan spoke back in the same calm tone.

"That's pretty good, Jimmy. If I ever need someone to write my biography I know who to call."

"Good one, Coast. And the title of that book is up to you, pal. Should we call it, *The Long and Happy Life of Dan Coast*, or maybe, *The Horrible, Painful Death of a Smartass Who Took Off with Another Man's Wife?*" Jimmy asked.

"Way too long. The publisher would never go for it. Let's hold off on the title for a while, Jimmy. Let's just call it a work in progress for now."

"Sure, we'll hold off on the title, but let me explain the next chapter to you." Jimmy's voice had taken on a flinty quality; the bantering was done. "Dan and Paula climb into Dan's Porsche tomorrow afternoon around three. You should be back from your fishing trip by then. Yeah, I know about that too. They drive up to Islamorada. They pull into Sid's Beach Bar and Grill around six-thirty. Dan parks, Paula gets out of the car, and Dan drives away. Jimmy doesn't kill Dan."

Dan opened his mouth to speak. The phone went dead.

"Dammit, he hung up. I had a good comeback about editing that chapter I think he would have enjoyed," Dan said, putting down the phone. He sank his head back into the frayed back of his La-Z-Boy and stared at the ceiling.

"Looks like someone lost the mood," Paula said, poking Dan's crotch with her finger.

"Yeah, *Little* Dan's exhausted," Dan said. "And so am I. I'm going to bed."

They walked down the hall together. Dan walked into his bedroom, Paula on his heels. Dan stopped, turned, put his hands on Paula's shoulders, turned her around, and gently pushed her out the door, shutting and locking it behind her.

"Maybe tomorrow?" Paula called out through the door.

Dan said nothing.

"Okay then, rain check."

Chapter Ten

Dan awoke on his back, staring up through the slowly spinning blades of the ceiling fan, at the white beadboard ceiling. His alarm hadn't gone off yet, that radio wouldn't play for another ten minutes. His head hurt, his eyes burned. A few drinks had turned into a few drinks too many. That, added to a night filled with visions of mob hits, scenes from *The Godfather*, and the cast of *The Sopranos* all holding guns to his head, made for a poor night's sleep. They say you can't die in your dreams. That may be true, but you can still feel the cold cement as it fills the bucket around your feet, and you can almost taste the salt water as you sink down lower and lower as you begin your eternal sleep with the fishes.

He lay there on his pillow, fingers clasped behind his head, staring upward, wishing he had taken a few aspirins before he went to bed, or had drunk a few glasses of water,__ both tricks a drinker uses to diminish the next morning's symptoms of the night before. Dan remembered doing these things as a teenager. The water and the aspirins, along with a giant bowl of Lucky Charms, sometimes did the trick. He knew that the times it worked were probably just the nights he hadn't drunk enough, but everyone has their rituals, baseball players, musicians, and even drunks.

"… mmy Buffett's 'Last Mango in Paris.' It's six o'clock, and it's going to be a beautiful day in paradise," came Tiny's voice from the radio. *Chuck on vacation?* Dan wondered. "The current temperature is seventy-eight with a high of eighty-nine today. Light winds out of the west at five to ten miles per hour. Coming up we have the Zac Brown Band, Bruce Springsteen, and Gordon Lightfoot's *The Wreck of the Edmund Fitzgerald* right here on the Florida Keys' official radio station US-1, 104.1."

Dan rolled over and smacked the snooze button with the palm of his hand, returned to his pre-alarm position, and let out a big sigh. He liked Gordon Lightfoot, but who wanted to hear about the wreck of the *Edmund Fitzgerald* right before a fishing trip. That would be about like watching *Airport* right before a long flight.

"I just wanted to go fishing," He whispered to himself. *And how did he even know I was going fishing?* Dan wondered.

He threw his legs over the side of the bed and stood up with a groan, and the usual snaps and cracks.

As he walked down the hall he gently pushed open the guest room door to check on his new roommate. He pulled the door closed quietly. Dan learned a lot about Paula the previous day, and already this morning he learned a few things too. One: She slept in the nude, on top of the sheets, and with a nightlight. And two: Judging from the lack of tan lines, she also sunbathed in the nude.

Dan made his coffee, sipped it. Staring at his fishing pole in the corner by the back door, he wondered what to do next. The fishing pole only moved from its spot about six times a year. Dan wasn't a die-hard fisherman, but Red was, and so was Phil. Dan went along on the trips just for the camaraderie…, and the booze. Dan was the type of fisherman that could get his line snagged on a branch in the middle of the ocean. He was lucky if he caught one fish to Red and Phil's four, but they were lucky if they could drink one beer to Dan's four.

After retrieving the morning edition of the *Key West Citizen* and pouring a second cup of coffee, Dan walked out the back door and down the gravel pathway to the two Adirondack chairs by the fire pit. As he sat down he heard the slamming of a screen door from the house next door. Dan turned to look.

"You're up early!" Bev shouted from her back deck, the deck Dan had recently built.

It was a small deck, about ten by eight, with three steps to the ground. Just big enough for a couple chairs and a gas grill. Bev had wanted her husband Frank to build her a deck for years. He had always promised to, thinking he had all the time in the world. He didn't. In the few years since Frank's death, however, it was Dan who tried to fulfill some of those promises. The new front door, shutters, an outdoor water faucet, and now the deck were all his handy work.

"Yeah, too early," Dan returned. "Coffee?" he asked, holding his cup in the air.

Bev held up her own cup, then turned and pulled open her back door to let Buddy out, and then walked over to Dan's to join him, with Buddy prancing closely behind, his tongue nearly dragging the ground.

Dan eyed the mutt with his usual grudging affection. "I wondered where that dog went to. I was hoping maybe he packed up and moved back home."

Upstate New York was the back home that Dan was referring to. Even though he had moved to the Keys over

70

four years ago, he still considered New York his home. His family was there; his old friends were there; he had a small storage unit there; and his wife was buried there.

Bev folded her arms across her chest and said, "This is your home, Dan, and it's Buddy's home too. Just accept it."

Dan looked over the top of his paper at Bev and then down to his dog. Buddy gave him a goofy dog grin and, after turning around three times, settled down at Dan's feet with a noise that was half sigh, half burp.

"I'm supposed to be going fishing this morning with Phil, but something came up, Dan said. "Now I don't know what to do."

"What came up?" Bev asked, as she sat down in the empty chair.

"A Mafia princess came up."

"What's that supposed to mean?"

"You've heard of Big Jimmy Pantucco?"

"Yeah. I read the papers. I watch the news. He's some kind of big Mafia guy, right?"

"Not too big, but big enough."

Bev rolled her eyes and shook her head. "Dan, Dan, Dan," she clucked, what did you get yourself into this time?"

"Long story short, I stopped to have lunch at a little diner on my way home from Miami yesterday. Turns out it was owned by Jimmy Pantucco. I'm sitting there having a drink, him and his wife are having an argument, she disappears. When I go out to my car, she's sitting in the front seat. Asks me to help her. She asks me to drive away. So I did."

"Smart move."

"It seemed like a good idea at the time."

"How could it seem like a good idea at the time?"

"Because, at the time, I didn't know he was Big Jimmy Pantucco, and she was kind of hot."

Bev raised her cup of coffee to Dan. "Well it's been nice knowing you neighbor."

"He called here last night. Wants her back at six thirty tonight. Now I don't know what to do."

"I'd make damn sure I had her back at six-twenty nine tonight."

"No, I mean about the fishing trip. Should I go, should I not go?"

Bev nearly did a spit take. "That's what you're worried about, a goddamn fishing trip?"

"Well, hell, I've been looking forward to it," Dan shrugged.

"Grow up!" Bev said as she got up and headed toward Dan's back door for another cup of coffee.

"You're no help at all," Dan grumbled as he followed Bev in through the door and into the kitchen.

As the two walked into the kitchen, they were surprised to see a very naked Paula, bent over and rummaging inside the refrigerator. She heard the back door slam, stood up, and turned around.

"Oh, hi. I thought you were on a fishing trip," Paula said.

"Bev, Paula. Paula, Bev," Dan introduced the two women.

"It's a pleasure to meet you," Paula said, reaching out one hand as she did her best to cover the upper half of her body with the other.

Huh, Dan thought, *covering up the top instead of the bottom. I gotta ask someone about this.*

"Likewise," Bev said with a raised eye brow, also extending a hand. "Maybe you should go put something on before you catch cold, dear."

"Yeah from the looks of it, that fridge is throwing off some pretty cold air," Dan said grinning.

After Paula closed the door and headed back to her room, Bev shot Dan a disgusted look.

"What is she, seventeen? Ya sick bastard."

"Actually, she's twenty-three, and I didn't touch her. She couldn't keep her hands off *me,* though."

"Yeah, I bet. That must have pretty rough on you."

After Paula had returned, fully dressed, Dan explained to her exactly what was said during last night's phone call with Big Jimmy, and told her she had till he got back from fishing to decide what she was going to do.

Dan said his good-byes to the two women, grabbed his fishing pole and a small blue cooler with a New York Yankees emblem on the side, and headed out the back door and around the gravel path to his car. Paula walked to the cupboard and grabbed the box of Pop-Tarts.

"That's not what you're planning on eating for breakfast, is it?" Bev asked Paula.

"It's either these or Corn Flakes," Paula answered.

"Frosted Flakes," Dan said.

Bev ignored Dan and said, "Well, now, you just come right on over to my house and I'll fix you a nice breakfast, a real breakfast, eggs and bacon, and we'll have a little girl talk."

Chapter Eleven

Dan's Porsche pulled into Island Adventures at six fifteen. Fifteen minutes late, right on the dot.

Phil Lambert, one of Dan's closest friends on the island, and the owner of Island Adventures, was not so patiently awaiting Dan's arrival. Phil was leaning up against his truck, dressed in Lee denim cutoffs, an old Kansas City Chiefs jersey, and an unzipped fishing vest. Sitting proudly on top of his head was an old fishing hat covered in flies and hooks, and on his feet were white Converse low-tops and white tube socks, with two red stripes around the top. Phil stood there shaking his head and looking at his watch as Dan skidded to a stop.

"Jesus Christ! What are you wearing?" Dan said, climbing from his car. "You look like Albert Lewis and Colonel Henry Blake had a baby."

"It's my lucky fishing outfit, ya douche. I'll have you know I've caught a lot of fish in this outfit," Phil said.

"What do you do, hit them in the head with a club while they're bent over laughing?"

"Laugh all you want, but April told me I look just like I did in high school."

Dan chuckled. "I don't think she meant it as a compliment."

"Oh yeah? I caught *her* while dressed like this too."

Dan pulled his fishing pole from the car, along with the small cooler. He had packed the cooler with ice and six bottles of Coke he had bought at the Corner Grocery Store on Bertha Street. He had also purchased a bottle of Bacardi Rum. Standing by his car, he opened each Coke bottle, poured out the equivalent of three shots, added three shots of rum to each bottle, and placed each cap back on the bottles. He then placed each bottle back into the cooler.

The two men walked down the dock toward Phil's boat. Dan jumped from the dock to the deck of the boat. Phil starting to do the same, hesitated, thought better of it, and then put his foot on the side rail and stepped in.

"Boys, boys!" Came a voice from behind them.

They turned to see Phil's wife, April, on her way down from the office with a small plastic container.

"You forgot the cookies I made for you," April said, handing the cookies to Phil.

"Thanks, hon," Phil said, taking the cookies.

"What kind of cookies?" Dan asked.

"Pumpkin cookies. Your favorite, Dan," April replied.

Dan liked April because she was comfortable in her own skin. She wasn't a raging beauty, she knew it, and she didn't care, which made her other charms, her quick wit, her easy going manner, her thoughtfulness, all the more attractive. In a town like Key West, where everybody wanted to be known as an eccentric character, April was content to be a good wife to Phil and a good person to everyone else. Dan admired that, and he respected April more than just about any woman he had ever known.

"Hey, April, if something terrible happens on this fishing trip," Dan teased her, "and only one of us comes back alive, and it's not Phil, will you marry me?

"No," April replied with a wink, "you're not man enough for a woman like me, Dan."

"It's my lack of tube socks, isn't it, April?" Dan asked.

"No, it's your lack of tube steak," Phil interjected. "Now shut the hell up and get that line untied. I have to be back by one to take another group out."

"Can't Derrick take them out?" Dan asked, as he untied the two nylon ropes that tethered the boat to the dock.

"Derrick doesn't work here anymore. We had a little problem the other day. I had to let him go."

"I heard about the trouble. I didn't know you fired him."

"I had no choice, Dan," Phil said somberly. From his tone Dan decided it wasn't a subject he wanted to pursue right now.

Phil gently pushed the throttle forward on his 2005, thirty-three foot Grady-White as they pulled away from the dock and out to sea. With one hand on the wheel and the other on the throttle Phil turned to Dan and grinned, then pushed the throttle all of the way forward. The twin Yamahas roared and the front of the boat lifted out of the water. The two men grinned from ear to ear like two school boys admiring a friend's new bike.

"They say money can't buy you happiness, old buddy, but ever since I bought this boat, I can't stop grinning," Phil yelled over the wind and engine noise.

"Can I drive, can I drive?" Dan cried.

"Can't. My mom said no one else can drive it."

Both men laughed. Dan opened a can of beer for Phil and handed it to him. Phil placed it in the cup holder to his left. Then Dan opened a rum and Coke for himself.

Phil stood in front of the captain's chair, both hands on the steering wheel. Dan stood in front of the co-pilots chair, one hand resting over the wind shield. In his other hand was the rum and Coke. Both men were wearing sun glasses, and the wind was blowing through their hair as the boat bounced along the waves toward what was sure to be a great day of fishing.

Phil was thinking only of fishing.

Dan was thinking of everything but fishing.

Chapter Twelve

"It's only one thirty, Derrick, she doesn't start work till three … I don't know … no … yes … I haven't seen her since she left last night … I don't know … I don't know … Okay … Bye."

Red shook his head as he hung up the phone. Dan had come into the bar halfway through the conversation.

"It was Derrick," Red said.

"I figured," Dan said.

"Cindy didn't come home last night."

"I got that."

"I hope nothing's wrong."

"Me too."

"Should I do something?"

"Yeah."

"What?" Red asked.

"Make me a drink," Dan said.

Red grimaced, shook his head, and turned to make Dan a drink. He didn't have to ask what he wanted to drink. It was always the same; tequila, Seven, and lime. As predictable as 007 and his cockamamie vodka martini, shaken, not stirred. But that was what Red liked about Dan; he was as reliable as the sunrise, and his couldn't-give-a-shit demeanor masked a heart of gold. If Red had to be stranded on a desert island for six months with anybody on earth, it would be Dan Coast, Dan Coast and an earplug for his one good ear.

Red slid the drink across the bar to Dan, the glass leaving a trail of moisture in its wake. Dan grabbed it. He took the lime off the side of the glass, squeezed it between his fingers, and let the juice drip into the glass. He stirred it with the swizzle stick, removed the stick and laid it on the bar. He took a drink.

"Ahhh, that's good," he said. "I haven't had a drink in about twenty five minutes."

Red grinned. "That must be some kind of record."

"That's not true. I once went thirteen years without drinking."

Red looked up from wiping down the bar. "What happened to make you start drinking after thirteen years?"

"I turned fourteen."

Both men laughed.

Dan's phone rang. He pulled it from his pocket and answered it. "Hello."

"Hi, sweetheart," said Paula on the other end.

Dan rolled his eyes. "It's *sweetheart* now?"

"Yes, sweetheart," replied Paula, affecting a syrupy Southern belle accent. "What time are you going to be home?"

"Home? You mean *my* home? I'll be there in about an hour. I'm at Red's, having a few drinks."

"Okay. I'm almost home. I picked up some steaks at the grocery store. We're going to cook out over to Bev's tonight for supper, so don't eat at Red's. You can invite him too, if you want. Also, I picked up a bottle of tequila for you. I figure if I get you drunk enough tonight, maybe I'll get lucky."

Dan, ever the frugal gourmet, did some quick addition in his head. "Where the hell did you get the money for all that stuff?"

"Your top dresser drawer, sweetie."

"Swell. Hey, have you seen Cindy today? She didn't go home last night."

"Yes, I did. I had breakfast with her this morning. She stayed at Bev's last night."

"Okay, I'll be home in … I'll be to *my* home in a little while," Dan said, hanging up his phone.

"The little lady?" Red asked. He enjoyed watching Dan squirm just a little, and his shit-eating grin didn't hide that fact.

"It might as well be," Dan sighed. "She's been here for two days, and she already tells me where, what, and when I'm going to eat, and who I can invite. She's got this crazy way of making people do whatever she asks, including me. She also stole money out of my dresser to pay for the dinner. She walks around the house wearing next to nothing. She's all over me."

"Must be rough," Red said in his best sarcastic tone.

"It is, trust me. Hit me again," Dan said, sliding his empty glass back the same way it had come.

"So who?" Red asked.

"Who *what*?" Dan replied irritably.

"Who are ya gonna invite to dinner?"

"You want to come to dinner, Red?"

"What time?"

"An hour after I've finished my last drink here. Now make me another tequila, Seven, and lime."

"Whatever you say, 007

Chapter Thirteen

Dan turned onto Beach View Street. The top was down. Kenny Chesney was singing "Flip Flop Summer." There wasn't a cloud in the sky, but the DJ had just said rain was on the way. Dan had one hand draped casually over the steering wheel and the other hanging over the door. He sang along with Kenny, tapping his fingers on the door to the beat of the music. He smiled as he got closer to home.

Quit smiling ya moron. She's someone else's wife. She's too young. She drives you nuts. Her husband is going to kill you.

He told himself all these things, but yet he still couldn't wait to get home and see her. He had seen the effect she had on other men, and he told himself it would never work on him. Yet it was working. It just took a little longer for someone so cynical, someone who usually kept their guard up.

Dan turned into his driveway and got out of the car. He noticed the damage to the front steps from the night before. *Watch out for sharks*, he thought, and smiled. He walked down the gravel path to the back steps. *I should really plant something in those flower boxes next week.* Dan stopped and looked around his yard. He could hear the raucous calls of the seagulls, and the waves pounding the beach. He looked at the hammock that hung between two palm trees. He looked at the fire pit, and the two Adirondack chairs. *Master of all I survey*, he thought a little smugly. *It ain't New York, and it ain't much, but it's all I need.* This was Dan's little slice of Paradise USA, and it was perfect, except for a little fly in the ointment named Paula.

He looked over toward his neighbor's house. Buddy was running around Bev's yard with a stick in his mouth. Bev was chasing him. She looked over and waived to Dan. Dan took a deep breath, held it for a moment, and let it out. He ran his fingers through his hair, turned, and proceeded up the steps. He pulled open the screen door.

"Honey, I'm home!" he called out sarcastically.

There was no answer. He stepped back, opened the door, and looked over toward Bev's. She was throwing the stick over Buddy's head toward the beach.

"Paula over there?" Dan called out.

Bev was bent over, slapping her knees in encouragement as Buddy retrieved the stick from the surf and trotted back to her.

"Good boy, Buddy! No, haven't seen her since she left for the store," Bev answered back, pulling the stick from Buddy' slobbery mouth.

Dan closed the door behind him. He saw a bottle of tequila on the counter, as well as a stack of about six steaks wrapped in clear plastic, and two bags of salt potatoes. He noticed something spattered on the cupboard door. He walked over. He rubbed it with his finger. It was dry. It was brown. Dan knew right away it was blood. Dan's nostrils flared as a pungent, metallic smell like an old paper sack of ten-penny nails left out in the rain came to his nose. The telltale aroma of dried blood, the floor was covered with it. He slowly turned toward the door leading into the living room. He walked over and peered through the doorway.

There was a woman. She was sitting in a chair, facing toward him. She had a plastic grocery bag over her head. The bag was white, with red letters. "Winn-Dixie" it read, upside down. Wrapped around her neck was duct tape. Her head was tilted back. Her hands were taped behind her.

"No," Dan whispered quietly; then he yelled it, "NO!" as he quickly moved toward her.

He grabbed the bag with both hands ripping it open. Her head fell forward. Thick red blood ran from the bag and through his fingers. He lifted her head, brushed back her hair. It was Paula, her face smeared with blood. Her skin was split open above her right eye, revealing a skull that had been dented and cracked. Something-not-blood was seeping from the crack. Dan let go of her. Paula's head fell back again. Her eyes were open. The life that once occupied those eyes was gone.

Dan took a step back. He looked at his blood covered hands. He wiped his hands on his shirt and looked at them again. Still stained he wiped them again more vigorously.

Dan heard his screen door creak. "What's the matter? I heard you yell," Bev said, as she entered the back door, Buddy at her side.

Dan turned, to prevent her from seeing Paula. He was too late. She ran into the living room.

"Omigod!" she cried out. "Omigod!"

Dan threw his arms around Bev and pulled her back into the kitchen.

Bev was yelling, "Why, why?"

Dan pulled Bev close and held her.

Chapter Fourteen

Dan stood in his front yard with his arm around Bev. It was a little after seven, and the sun was shining low in the sky through a crack in the clouds. A slight mist hung in the air after the afternoon rain. Bev, looked downward with her hands over her face, sobbing. Dan watched as two paramedics wheeled the gurney that held Paula's body, zipped tightly in an olive green body bag, down the gravel pathway to a waiting ambulance parked in the street. Both men nodded to Dan as they walked by. They knew him; Key West, after all, was a small town and almost everybody knew everybody else. Dan nodded back. The nods are usually followed by a "How ya doin?" or "What's up?" But not tonight. It was obvious how everyone was doing.

There was a cop car sitting sideways in the street about thirty yards away to block traffic, and another one approximately the same distance away at the other end of the street. The light bars on top of both vehicles were strobing and lighting up half the neighborhood. The police chief's car was parked on Dan's lawn. His lights were also on.

A few police officers walked around Dan's property, as well as the yards of the neighboring homes. They knocked on the doors of the people who weren't already standing in their front yards watching the show. They talked with passersby. They shined their flashlights around and searched the ground for anything that might constitute a clue. Rick Carver, the chief of police, was inside with two plain clothes detectives, the county coroner, and a police photographer.

The paramedics slowly pushed the gurney into the ambulance and closed the door. The men conferred briefly about something and climbed through their respective doors. Dan and Bev watched motionless as the ambulance drove away.

Dan heard his screen door open and looked toward his house. The photographer exited the front door, got in his car, and left. He was soon followed by the coroner. A few moments later Chief Carver also came out, and walked over to Dan and Bev.

"So, why don't you explain to me exactly how the wife of Big Jimmy Pantucco ended up *living* in your house," Rick said, "and then *dying* in your house."

"It's a long story," Dan said.

Rick folded his beefy arms over his substantial gut. Entwined, they looked like two boa constrictors mating. "I got all night."

"Can I head home, Rick?" Bev asked. "I'm not feeling that well, I want to lie down."

"Sure, Bev. I'll stop over some time tomorrow and see you. I have a few questions to ask you. Don't leave town."

"Where would I be going?" she whispered to Dan as she turned and walked away.

Rick called out to one of the officers nearby to walk Bev home and make sure she got there okay. He grabbed another detective by the arm as he walked by. "Put out an APB on James Pantucco, AKA, Big Jimmy Pantucco, AKA Jimmy P." The detective nodded and kept walking.

"AKA, I think I'd like to sit down too, Rick," Dan said smirking.

Rick shook his head. "I don't want anyone in the house yet. Wait till the guys are done inside. Let's go around back and have a seat together. You can tell me the story of how you stole a mob wife."

The two men walked together around the back of the house and down the gravel pathway to the two Adirondack chairs next to the fire pit. Rick sat first, removing a note pad from a compartment in his leather duty belt, which Dan had always thought rivaled Batman's in its array of cool doodads.

"I always wanted one of those when I was a kid," Dan said, pointing at Rick's belt. "Would you mind if I played with the batarang while we talked?"

"I'm not in the mood tonight, Dan. How about if you just start from the beginning."

Dan shrugged his shoulders, sat down in the other chair, and began his story. "It was a dark and stormy night..."

"Listen, smartass, I said I wasn't in the mood," Rick said through clenched teeth.

Dan grinned. "Sorry. Let me start again. I was on my way back here from Miami. It wasn't a dark and stormy night. It was lunch time."

"What were you doing in Miami?"

"That doesn't matter."

"It might matter to me."

"It doesn't matter to me that it might matter to you. Do you want me to go on or not?"

"Go ahead."

"Like I said, I was on my way back here from Miami. I stopped at a little bar and grill in Islamorada, right off the highway. Two folks I took to be the bartender and a waitress were having a little argument. Nothing too heavy, but it lasted most of the time I was there. About the time I was getting ready to leave, she disappears."

Rick looked up from his scribbling. "She?"

"The waitress ... or who I thought was the waitress__"

"What is it with you and waitresses?"

Dan glared at Rick. "When I get out to my car, she's laying down, curled up in the passenger seat, holding on to a small bag. She asks me to get her out of there. So I did. It wasn't till we got back here that I found out she wasn't just some waitress. She was Jimmy P.'s wife, and the bartender was actually Jimmy P. As in Big Jimmy Pantucco."

"Is it because they laugh at all of your stupid jokes? Said Rick, revisiting his earlier question. "They get paid to laugh at your stupid jokes, same as they get paid to bring you your stupid food. It's a package deal. They probably don't think you're funny."

Dan ignored Rick's inane line of questioning (inspired, he knew, by Rick's jealousy of his ladies' man reputation) and finished his story, purposely leaving out the history of violence on Jimmy's part, and the part about the phone call from Jimmy saying he wanted his wife back today at six-thirty. It was now seven-fifteen. Not only was

Jimmy not getting his wife back, but he was also never going to see her again. Dan wondered just how angry Jimmy would be, and just who would feel the brunt of that anger ... and, do fish really sleep?

"So, why did you let her stay here? Why didn't she get a hotel room?" Rick asked.

"She didn't have any money. I told her she could stay here for a few days till she figured out what she was going to do next."

"And what was she going to do next?"

Dan watched a gull swoop down and pluck an unsuspecting something from the sea. "Someone didn't give her quite enough time to figure that one out, now did they?"

Just then two detectives exited through Dan's back door and walked toward Rick.

"We're going to take off, chief. I think we got all we need here," one of the detectives said.

"Yeah, you guys head out. I'll catch up with you at the station," Rick replied.

"Can I go back in my house now?" Dan asked.

"Yeah, go ahead. I'm gonna take off too, looks like I have a gangster to find. If I have any questions later I'll give you a call ... Oh, and ... don't leave town."

Dan had to bite his tongue. *"Don't leave town," he says again. I thought I watched too much television. He should have that phrase carved on his head stone.*

"I wasn't planning on going anywhere, Rick," Dan replied.

"See that you don't. I don't want you running back up to Islamorada to talk to a certain bartender before I do ... because if you do, I'll arrest you for interfering with an ongoing investigation. Remember, I'm the cop, you're not."

Rick paused for a moment, trying to think of something suitably snide. He knew Dan fancied himself an armchair detective and said, "You're not even a *private* cop."

"But I play one on TV," Dan deadpanned.

Rick followed the detectives out to the front of the house. Dan also followed. He walked out into the middle of his yard and watched as Rick, the detectives, and the other police officers climbed back into their cars and drove off, one by one. The street was once again quiet.

Dan stood alone in his yard. He looked up one side of the street and down the other. *The streets back to normal. No one would ever guess a murder had taken place a few short hours before.* Dan looked down at the deep, muddy tire tracks spoiling the looks of his front yard. *I wonder if the city will pay to have that fixed?*

Dan noticed Mrs. McGee, with her curtain pulled back, looking out her front window at him from across the street. She, like Bev, was also a widow. Dan didn't know too much else about her. He knew she moved here from Fort Lauderdale. He knew her husband was involved in marine salvage, whatever that was, and that he died back in the mid-eighties. She had a step daughter named Jean who was a veterinarian up north, Ohio or Michigan, maybe. She baked a mean Christmas cookie. She was a very nice woman, polite. She reminded Dan of the mom from The Partridge Family, only without the psychedelic bus and the gaggle of kids. Almost everyone reminded Dan of someone from television. Dan didn't know if Edna McGee played the keyboards. He doubted it.

They stared at each other for a few seconds. Dan lifted his hand to wave hello, but she let the curtain drop too soon and didn't notice. He put his hands back in his pockets. He was all alone again. Well, almost alone. Buddy walked slowly up to Dan's side and, with a sad whimper, lay down beside him.

"Part of me is wondering how you got that bag over her head, Buddy," Dan said, looking straight ahead.

Dan turned and went back into the house. He stood in the middle of his living room. The picture of his wife that sat on the small table next to Buddy's bed had been tipped over. Dan walked over and stood it back up. The cops had taken the dining room chair Paula had died in. There was blood on the floor where it had sat. He walked into the kitchen. There was still dried blood on the kitchen floor, as well as the counter top. The steaks were still there. Dan picked them up and threw them in the trash.

The screen door opened. It was Red, a six pack of Bud Lite Lime in one hand and a bag of Cheetos in the other.

"Sorry I'm late, pal," he apologized. "Something came up at the bar. Did you eat yet?

Dan didn't answer; he just looked down and shook his head.

"Wow, who died?" he said jovially, "I feel more like I'm at a funeral than a party."

His jaw dropped when he saw the bloodstained floor.

Chapter Fifteen

"Sorry," Red said after Dan filled him in. "I didn't hear anything about it."

"Yeah, what are ya gonna do?" Dan replied.

The two men walked along the beach with Buddy trotting at their heels. Dan told Red the parts he had left out while giving his statement to Rick. Dan threw a tennis ball into the water as they walked. Tongue flapping wildly, Buddy would run into the water and bring it back each time.

"That goddam dog comes back every time," Dan remarked. "I wonder who taught him to swim." Dan harbored an unfair grudge against the mutt for his part in his wife's death, a grudge that his fondness for the dog usually overcame.

"He loves you," Red replied, laughing.

"Yeah."

"So, what do you think is going to happen next?" Red asked.

"I don't know. A dog like this could live another eight or nine years."

"I mean about Jimmy Pantucco, ya idiot," Red said, shaking his head.

"Simple. He's gonna kill me."

"Why would he kill *you*, if he's the one that killed *her*?"

"Just to make it look like he didn't."

Red was incredulous. "Bag over the head? Duct-taped to a chair? That screams Mafia hit. There's no one that won't believe he did it."

Dan looked his friend in the eyes. "*I* don't think he did it."

"Why not?"

"Because, it looks *too* much like a mob hit."

Red scratched his head. "Uh, don't mob hits usually look like mob hits?"

"Only when they're trying to send a message, when they want someone to know who it was. If they don't want anyone to know who did it, then it doesn't look like a mob hit. These guys aren't stupid. *These* bad guys are usually smarter than the good guys. Why do you think it takes years to build a case against one of them?"

"On *The Sopranos* it always looks like a mob hit," Red insisted.

Dan sighed. "I never thought I would say this, but this ain't TV, and let's stop saying mob hit!"

"Okay, okay! So how are ya gonna find out who did it?"

"I'm not. That's the cops' job."

Red looked crushed. "So you're not going to do *anything*?"

"What do you want me to do? No one hired me to find out. I'm not a cop. I'm not even a PI yet, for Chrissakes."

"What do you mean, 'yet'?"

"Nothing. Just a figure of speech." Dan answered. He didn't want Red to know about the brochures and pamphlets he had picked up in Miami. Dan was never the type to give up too much information, even to his closest friend. There was nothing worse than telling someone about your big plans and then not following through with them, and then spending the next two years explaining why.

By now the two men were back at Dan's fire pit. The sun was down, and the light was almost gone. It was cooling off, and there was a gentle breeze coming off the water.

"Why don't you build a fire?" Red suggested. "I'll go in and make us a couple drinks."

Dan went over to the small woodpile next to his shed and filled his arms with five or six pieces of fire wood, and brought them back to the pit. He went back to the shed and grabbed an old issue of the *Citizen* from a teetering stack of papers, crumpled up each page, and threw them into the pit, placing the fire wood on top. Smaller pieces first and then the larger. He pulled a Zippo lighter from his pocket. He looked at the inscription on the side. *To a pirate looking at 40. Love always, your 1st. Mate.* He flipped open the lid and lit the papers. Dan closed the lighter and squeezed it in his fist feeling it's warmth, then shoved it back in his pocket.

"Here ya go," Red said, handing Dan his drink.

"Thanks," Dan said, and sat down. He stretched out his legs in front of him and rested his head on the back of the chair, looking up toward where the stars should have been. *God damn clouds.*

"I thought I heard someone out here," Bev called out from her back deck.

"We got room for one more," Red yelled back.

"Let me throw on some flip-flops," she called back. "I'll be right over."

A few moments later Bev walked up to the fire. She was wearing pajama bottoms and top, and a sheer green robe; so long it trailed along the sand like a bridal train. She had a glass of red wine in one hand and a small radio in the other. She turned on the radio and tuned it in to 104.1, set it down on the ground next to the other chair, and sat down. Red walked to the shed and grabbed an aluminum folding chair with green webbing, unfolded it and sat down. The chair creaked under his girth.

"Hulk sit down!" Dan chided.

"Shut up, dickhead," Red shot back. "I didn't know they still made these things."

"We didn't wake you up did we, Bev?" Dan asked.

Bev was still chuckling from the Hulk reference and wiping the spilt wine from her chin. "No, I was just watching TV. Three hundred channels and two hundred and fifty of them have a reality show on. What the hell do I care what's in some storage unit? Or what some idiot left in his suit case? And do they really expect me to believe that that's what happens when some jamoke comes to repo your car? It's crazy." Bev cut herself off when she realized the rant had gone on too long and that Dan and Red were staring.

"Why don't you tell us how you really feel," Red said.

"Did you get some rest, Bev?" Dan jumped in.

"I didn't really need to lie down earlier. I just told Chief Carver that so he wouldn't ask me any questions. I wanted to have time to talk to you before I talked to him."

Dan perked up. "Talk to me? Why, what's the matter?"

Bev lowered her voice to a conspiratorial level. "I didn't want to tell him that I saw Derrick White leave your house about a half hour before you got home."

"Derrick White? Why was he at my house?

"He must have thought Cindy stayed at your house last night and came over to look for her," Red put in.

Bev nodded her agreement, then turned to Dan. "Derrick's a good boy. He wouldn't have done this, and I didn't want to get him involved until you had time to talk to him." Bev said to Dan.

"It looks like he's already involved, but I'll call him first thing in the morning," Dan said. He leaned back in his chair and took the last sip of his drink. He shook the ice in the glass at Red. "Hulk make more drink?"

Chapter Sixteen

Dan Coast walked in slow motion through his back door. The house was dark and filled with a heavy mist. He could hear music playing. It was quiet music, as if in the distance, but yet in the same room. He walked across the kitchen floor to the counter top. There was a package wrapped in newspaper. He slowly unwrapped it. It was meat, rancid meat covered in maggots, other small insects, and worms. He was startled. He stepped back covering his nose and mouth with his hand. The smell was horrible. He felt nauseous.

The music stopped. A faint muffled voice came from the other room, "Help me, help me," the voice called out. Dan walked toward the voice, his feet sticking to the ground with every step. He felt as though he was walking in glue. Looking down, he noticed the floor was covered in blood. It was dark red, thick, and sticky, it covered the kitchen as well as the living room floor.

The music started again. It was a country song. *What is that song,* he thought, *it sounds familiar. I've heard it before.* He walked into the living room. There he saw

Paula, sitting in a chair. A plastic bag covered her head. He couldn't see her face, but somehow he knew who it was. He tore open the bag. Blood ran from the tear. Dan lifted her head; her face was covered in blood and maggots. She spoke; "Help me." He dropped her head and stumbled backwards, slipping in the blood and falling on his back. He sat up. She slowly lifted her head, but this time it was Dan's own wife, her eyes looking toward him, her face covered in blood.

Her mouth opened to speak.

"Answer the phone," Alex whispered.

*****

The crashing sound of a storm shutter hitting the side of the house brought Dan out of a sound sleep. He sat up quickly. His head and chest were covered in sweat. He looked around the room to orientate himself.

Just then the music started to play again. This time he recognized it. It was Paula's phone.

Dan leapt from his bed to search for the phone. He ran into the living room looking around franticly. The music stopped. He froze, waiting for it to start again. A few seconds passed and the ringing began again. *The kitchen.* Dan ran into the kitchen, skidding on the linoleum. It was coming from down low. He dropped to his knees. He looked under the stove and then the fridge. He slid the drip pan from under the fridge. There it was. He picked it up and answered. "Hello!" he said. But it was too late.

Dan hit the phone icon, and then hit "recent calls." There were four calls from the same number in the last three minutes. He then went back to two nights earlier. The numbers were the same. It was Jimmy Pantucco's number.

The message light was blinking, but Dan didn't know the code. *It would be nice to hear just how angry he was before he got here,* Dan thought. He stared at the phone for a few moments, and then dialed Jimmy's number back. Dan heard the ringback tone and grinned. It was the theme to *The Sopranos*. He shook his head and rolled his eyes.

"Where da fuck are you, bitch?" came the angry voice suddenly from the other end.

"I'm standing in my kitchen, Jimmy," Dan replied.

"Coast! Where's my wife? I thought I told you to have her back last night."

"She couldn't make it. She ... she was tied up with something," *God, that was lame, even for me. I need some new material.*

"What?"

"Nothing."

"I'm on my way to get her, asshole, and when I get there you're a dead man."

"I wouldn't come here if I was you, Jimmy."

"Why not?"

"Because Paula's dead Jimmy, and the cops think it was you who killed her."

"What ... dead ... how ... what do you mean dead? How can she be dead?" There seemed to be real sadness in Big Jimmy's tone before the uncouth goodfella in him resurfaced. "What did you do you piece of shit?"

"Listen, Jimmy, I didn't want to tell you over the phone, but I sure as hell didn't want to tell you to your face," Dan said.

"Oh my God … I gotta pull over. I think I'm gonna be sick."

"Jimmy, just listen to me. Whoever did this set it up to look like a mob hit. That's why they think it's you."

"And *you* don't think it's me?"

"No! I don't think you're that stupid. Now shut up and listen. Have you passed the Marathon Marina yet?"

"No. It's right up here on the right."

"When you get to it, pull in. Park your car in the marina parking lot and wait for me. I'll be there as quick as I can. What are you driving?"

"A black Caddy."

"Figures."

"What the hell is that supposed to mean, douche bag?

Chapter Seventeen

Dan sped along Roosevelt headed toward Island Adventures. Reaching for his cell phone, he dialed Red's number.

"Hey, meet me at Phil's," he said upon hearing Red's voice.

"Yeah sure, I'm not doing anything. It's not like I have a business to run or anything. Christ, Cindy hasn't shown up yet today. Her shift started at nine__"

"Can you just meet me there?"

"Why, what's up?"

"Jeez! Just meet me there as quick as you can." *Click.*

Dan swung right, just past the sign that read, ISLAND ADVENTURES - LAND, SEA, AIR. The Porsche fishtailed as it hit the loose stone of Phil and April Garvey's parking lot. Dan quickly turned into the slide and righted the vehicle just as Mr. Marion, his eleventh grade driver's ed teacher, had taught him. Sliding on gravel was not that much different than sliding on the snow and ice of Dan's native central New York. "Slowly turn into the slide," Mr. Marion would say, his booze breath from the night before filling the interior of the 1979 Ford Taurus. "Turn into the slide," he would say again, with the palm of his hand out stretched toward the dash board. He would wave his hand in a clockwise motion and then reverse it, as though he himself were steering the car with some kind of a Jedi mind trick passed down from Yoda to all driving instructors. "Now pull over up here in front of Dicky's Market, and someone run in and get me a tomato juice. This hangover is killing me."

Dan skidded to a stop, leaving ruts in the stone and piling up a small mound of gravel in front of each tire, just as Phil Garvey was exiting the office.

"Do you have to drive in here that fast?" Phil carped. "It messes up the parking lot."

"I don't have to, but it's a lot of fun. Why don't you just have it black topped?"

"Because black top costs a lot of money, and the stone looks more islandier."

"Is islandier even a word?" Dan asked as he climbed from his car.

"Yeah, it is. Coined by me. Now are you here just to bust my balls, or did you need something?" Phil asked the question but already knew the answer.

"Phil, I need to borrow your boat for a couple of hours."

"No can do, pal. I got a charter going out in forty-five minutes."

Dan grinned. "Not *the* boat. *Your* boat."

The boat Dan was referring to was not the boat Phil used for every day charters. He was referring to Phil's own private 2009 Cigarette thirty-nine foot Top Gun Unlimited.

It was Phil's Christmas present to himself last year. Phil didn't loan this boat out, mainly because it was his baby, but also in part because no one had been stupid enough to ask. That is, up until now.

"*My* boat?" Phil asked, staring slack-jawed at Dan.

"Keys?" Dan said, palm extended.

"Why me?" Phil asked God, as he spun around and returned to the office.

Phil was exiting the office as Red pulled into the parking lot driving his new Jeep Wrangler 4x4 convertible. The top was off, and Eddie Money was belting out "Give Me Some Water" at the top of his lungs, with Red singing along in an off-key voice that would make a stuffed dog howl. Red wasn't wearing a shirt as usual, which made most onlookers ask the question, "When did Sasquatch learn to drive?" He skidded to a stop. Phil rolled his eyes and shook his head.

"Whaddaya think?" Red said, climbing out of the expensive embodiment of his mid-life crisis.

"It's orange," Dan said.

"It's not orange," Red huffed. "It's Mango Tango Pearl."

"Looks like Cinderella's pumpkin coach to me," Phil observed.

"Jealous a-hole," Red shot back.

Dan followed Phil down the dock. Red, slipping on his shirt, headed to the office, toward the complimentary donut and coffee table he knew was awaiting him.

"Mornin', Ape," Red greeted April, as he came through the door."

"Donut, Red?"

"That's what I'm here for," Red said, grabbing three donuts, and opening the refrigerator for a Pepsi.

Red caught up with the other two men standing beside Phil's thirty-nine-foot, high performance, twin-engine phallic symbol.

"Be careful with her … please," Phil pleaded. "Just because it goes too fast, doesn't mean you have to drive it too fast."

"Sure thing," Dan reassured him. "I'll treat her like she's my own."

Phil thought of Dan's one-foot-in-the-grave Porsche. "That's what I'm afraid of."

Red walked up to the boat still singing, "Give Me Some Water." "Cause I'm killing men on the Mexican border," He blurted out.

"It's 'Cause I killed a man on the Mexican border', and did you leave any donuts for the paying customers?" Phil demanded, seeing Red's fist full of donuts.

"Sorry, I didn't have time to eat *breaktist,"* Red answered. "Besides, the sign says, Help Yourself."

"But it doesn't say, 'all you can eat buffet,'" Phil complained, pointing at Red's generous helping of powdered and sugared, golden fried goodness.

"If you two are done arguing over the etiquette of self-monitored breakfast treat consumption, I could use one of you on this rocket boat," Dan said.

Red took an exaggerated bite of one of the donuts, and appeared to enjoy it way too much as he stared at Phil with a powdered sugar-covered smile. He turned and climbed into the boat.

"Wipe your face, for Chrissakes; you look like Tony Montana at the end of Scarface," Dan said. He turned to Red and warned, "Hold on to your ass, and you might want to take off that ball cap," as he eased the throttle forward. The hum of the twin Mercury racing engines roaring to life nearly gave Dan serious wood.

"You break it, you bought it!" Phil yelled, but the Cigarette had already rocketed out of sight with its two giddy passengers. He knew the thing could top out at 117 mph. *Dear God*, he prayed, *please don't let those two yahoos push it that far!*

Phil turned around and walked back toward the office, head down, hands in pockets. "There goes 850 grand down the drain," he sighed.

Chapter Eighteen

Dan eased back on the throttle and guided the boat through the channel and into Boot Key Harbor.

"Shit, that was some ride," said Red, smoothing down his tousled hair with his hands and placing his hat back on his head. "Wouldn't mind havin' one of these babies myself. Course, I'd have to hit the lottery first."

Dan knew to keep his mouth shut when Red dropped hints about tapping into Dan's lottery win years ago. "Watch out for any cops," he said. "I'm sure they have an APB out on Jimmy by now."

Red kept an eye out while Dan radioed in their arrival to the harbor.

After securing the boat to the dock, Dan and Red cautiously headed toward the parking lot in search of Jimmy's black Cadillac.

"I gotta hit the bathroom," Red said, turning toward the office. "I'll catch up with you in a second. Be careful."

"I'm always careful," Dan replied.

Dan walked past the main office and into the parking lot looking from car to car. There was a red Ford pickup, a white Oldsmobile Intrigue, two BMWs, a green Jag, a few mini vans, a couple of SUVs, and even a pink Volkswagen Bug. There was no black Cadillac. Dan walked past each car looking at their license plates. Georgia, Florida, Florida, Alabama, New York, Florida. The pink Bug also had a Florida plate, and next to the plate on the rear bumper was a little green, white, and orange sticker that read "MOB WIFE."

Seriously? Dan thought. He walked around to the driver's side of the car. Cupping his hands over his eyes to shade them from the sun, he looked inside. The keys were in the ignition. There was an empty can of Diet Coke on the passenger side floor.

The palm of a very large hand came down on Dan's left shoulder at the same moment something jabbed into his right kidney.

"Don't move," a man's voice with a New York accent said quietly into Dan's ear.

Dan had no intention of moving. He didn't have to turn around; he knew who it was.

"I thought you drove down in a Caddy," Dan said.

"I lied," the voice said. "Are you alone?"

"No. You're here too, Jimmy"

"I told you that smart mouth was gonna get you killed."

"I just don't listen."

"You have about ten seconds to tell me why I shouldn't pull this trigger right here, right n__"

"You have about five seconds to convince me of the same thing," came Red's voice from behind Jimmy, cutting him off.

Jimmy was now experiencing the same sensation Dan had felt of something pressed firmly against his kidney. Jimmy froze.

"You're making a big mistake, scumbag," Jimmy said.

"Only if someone else is about to walk up behind *me*," Red said. "Now, reach around and put the gun on the roof of the car."

Ha, reach around, Dan thought.

Jimmy slowly did as he was told. Giving up his weapon wasn't a sign of weakness or fear on Jimmy's part. He had been in this business for a long time. He was smart and knew when to pick his battles. The only emotion Jimmy showed was his red face. It was a mean, angry, red face.

"You brought a gun?" Dan asked.

"No," Red said, holding up a gnarled tree branch from a nearby oak. "But I did pick up this branch over there."

Jimmy swung around quickly, and Red brought the branch down hard on Jimmy's skull. Jimmy hit the ground just as hard as the branch hit him.

Both men stood side by side looking down, still cringing, at the motionless lump of wise guy. Red tossed the branch back over under the tree where he had found it.

"Scary guy," Dan said.

"Yeah, I bet he's real good at scaring twenty-three-year old girls," Red said.

Dan crinkled his nose and sniffed the air. "Twenty-three-year old girls, hell, I think I shit myself a little."

"Well he doesn't look so tough now, does he?" Red said, nudging the unconscious Mafioso with his foot.

Dan picked up Jimmy's gun and slipped it under his shirt, sliding it in between his waist band and the small of his back. "Come on, help me lift this sack of shit," he said.

Dan and Red walked along the dock with Jimmy between them. Jimmy's left arm was around Dan's neck, and his right arm was around Red's. It looked like a scene from *The Godfather* meets *Weekend at Bernie's.*

Dan's Ray-Ban sunglasses were now on Jimmy, and Red's Cub's cap was covering the purple, lump protruding from the bald spot on Jimmy's head. Both men struggled to keep Jimmy upright as they made their way back to the boat.

"Hey, he all right?" the harbor master asked as they shuffled by.

"Yeah, sure," Dan said. "Our friend here had a bit too much to drink last night. We're just trying to get him back home."

Neither man made eye contact with the harbor master as they passed by.

Upon reaching the boat, Red laid Jimmy on his back on the dock. Dan climbed into the boat and grabbed Jimmy's feet, while Red held his hands and pulled him from the dock, and into the boat. Jimmy hit the deck with a meaty thud.

"Jeez!" Dan sighed. "I think that's the biggest thing we ever pulled into a boat, isn't it?"

"Nope. Remember that nurse from Portland?" Red laughed.

"Oh yeah. She *was* a little bigger. *Uglier* too."

"Hey, she had great personality. She sent me a Christmas card last year."

Both men were laughing uncontrollably, when Dan looked up and noticed a small crowd had started to gather.

"Is he dead?" one on-looker said.

"Maybe someone should call the cops," said another.

"We better get the hell outta here," Dan said gesturing toward the crowd, and starting the twin engines.

Chapter Nineteen

Dan had shut off the engines and brought the boat to rest about three miles off shore adjacent to Sugar Loaf Key. The sea was calm; there was a slight breeze and the boat set almost motionless in the water.

Dan stood between the captain's chair and the co-pilot's seat, facing the Cigarette's stern. He had his arms crossed and was looking down at Jimmy. Jimmy was wearing a blue and gray Hawaiian shirt, unbuttoned, over a white Fruit of the Loom wife beater, and a pair of khakis. A snarl of kinky black hair peeked out like a pubic bush gone horribly awry around the neck of his wife beater, and on the Mafioso's exposed belly, which was otherwise as white as a beached whale. Red was on one knee beside Jimmy, patting him down for any other weapons he might have on him.

"First time I ever frisked Bigfoot," said Red, wincing in distaste. "This fat *sumunobitch* could use some serious manscaping."

"Did you check all of the body cavities, Red?" Dan asked in amusement.

"All that I dared. Nothing. Just an empty shoulder holster."

Jimmy was starting to come around, moaning and groaning like a drunk after an all-nighter. He lay on the deck's green indoor/outdoor carpeting, turning his head toward each of his captors, eyes squinting in the bright afternoon sun, trying to put two and two together.

Suddenly as though someone at the controls flipped a switch, Jimmy quickly rolled to his knees, reaching under his arm for a gun that wasn't there. Looking up, he saw his own gun pointing back at him.

"Looking for this?" Dan asked.

Jimmy leaned back slowly and rested on the heels of his feet.

"You gonna kill me, smartass? Like you killed my wife?"

"If I was gonna kill you, I would have done it before you woke up, and then thrown you into the water. Listen, Jimmy, I didn't kill your wife. Paula was dead when I got there. Now are you gonna calm down?"

"Yeah, I'll calm down, but I'm gonna need some answers."

"We'll find the answers, Jimmy. You have my word on that."

"Can I have my gun back?"

"No" Dan said. "You *may* not have your gun back."

"Now be a good little goodfella and shut the hell up for a while," Red chimed in.

Turning toward the powerboat's bow, Dan slipped the gun into the small compartment over the steering wheel.

He then picked up a wrench lying next to it. Letting Jimmy think that the wrench was his gun, he tossed it over the bow and into the water.

Jimmy clapped himself in the head with both hands and whined. "Awe, come on! My dad gave me that pistol when I turned eighteen. Jesus, you didn't have to throw it over board."

"Sorry, I didn't know it had sentimental value. Your dad ever buy you a gun, Red?" Dan asked.

"No, but my mom bought me a bike for my birthday once, and some neighborhood kids threw it into Wolf Lake," Red replied, playing along. "So I know how he feels."

"Yeah, shitty," said Jimmy. He got up off the deck and sat on the bench at the rear of the boat. He leaned forward, resting his elbows on his knees, and ran his finger through his hair. He looked up at Dan.

"So what's next, tough guy?" he asked.

"Next," Dan said, "we get you to my place to hide out for a few days till we can prove you didn't kill Paula."

Dan turned and restarted the engines, pushed the two throttles forward, and aimed the boat toward home. Red grabbed furiously for his hat as the wind took it. He wasn't quick enough. He looked back as his Chicago Cubs baseball cap found its final resting place atop the ocean waves.

"Dan, can you tu__"

"No."

"Douche."

"Why are you doing this? What are you, some kind of private dick or something?" Jimmy yelled out over the roar of excessive horsepower.

"No," Red offered, "just a dick head. This is just some sick hobby he works at now and then. He watched way too much TV growing up. All those hours of *Cannon, Kojack, Columbo, Rockford Files, Magnum P.I.,* they warped his brain. Now he thinks he can solve crimes."

"I *have* solved a few crimes!" Dan hollered back.

Red looked at Jimmy and shook his head ruefully. "He caused a shootout in a hotel room that left three people dead, and me wounded. He was lucky enough to be sitting in the shitter once and overheard two guys planning a murder. And this one time this dame hired him to take pictures of her hubby banging his secretary for blackmail purposes. Oh yeah, and there was the time he put a camcorder on his front porch and solved the big caper of which neighbor's cat was shitting on his front lawn. So yeah, I guess he has solved a few crimes.

Dan's face had reddened a little by the end of Red's story, but he kept his eyes forward and said, "Dame? Suddenly you're Dixon Hill?"

Chapter Twenty

Red had talked Dan into letting him take over the controls and was easing the boat up to Phil's dock the best he could. His best wasn't good enough, however, and the sickeningly sound of fiberglass rubbing against aluminum could be heard over the low idle. All three men aboard made the same grimacing face. Red pushed the throttles forward a little and turned the boat around, facing the slight damage away from the dock.

"There," Red said, "ya can't see it from my house."

Dan tried not to laugh. He didn't try hard enough.

"Phil's gonna make you pay for that, you know," Dan said.

Red shrugged. "*You* borrowed it. Just pay for it out of your expense account."

"No one's paying me. I don't have an expense account."

"There's ten grand in it for ya … if ya find out who killed my wife," Jimmy put in, sounding eerily *Godfather*-like.

"Sounds like an offer I can't refuse," Dan said.

All three men walked up the dock toward Phil's office.

"I wonder where Phil is? I thought he would be right out here the minute he heard his boat pull in," Red said.

"Yeah, it's pretty quiet around here," Dan said, noticing the unusual silence.

Just then a small army of police rushed at them from all sides, guns drawn and aimed.

"Freeze, scumbags!" one of the cops ordered.

"On the ground! On the ground!" yelled another.

Cops ran up to each man and forced them to the ground face first. Each man had a knee in his back and was being handcuffed as Chief Rick Carver walked from the office. He had his usual *I'm so pleased with myself* swagger and expression on his face as he crammed one of Phil's free donuts into his mouth.

"Well, well, what do we have here?" Rick asked, removing his gold-framed aviator sunglasses as he sauntered toward them.

"What the he—"

"I'll ask the questions here, Coast," Rick cut him off. He breathed a heavy breath of hot air onto each lens of his sunglasses, and with his shirt between his thumb and finger, wiped them clean. He put them back on with great ceremony, relishing being the center of attention.

Phil and April exited the office and sprinted toward the crowd of cops. Dan, Red, and Jimmy were now on their knees, legs crossed behind them, as instructed by the officers, and their hands cuffed behind them.

Dan fixed Phil in his hard gaze. "Thanks for the heads up, pal."

"Sorry, Dan, they wouldn't let me near the radio."

Rick walked up to Jimmy. "You must be Big Jimmy Pantucco," he said, looking down on his prize. "You don't look so big now, do ya?"

"My friends call me Jimmy P. I'd shake your han—"

"I'm not your friend!" Rick shot back.

"Maybe if you'd just get to know me," Jimmy said, grinning.

"I know you, and I know a lot of people just like you. You're under arrest, scumbag, for the murder of Paula Pantucco. Read him his rights, and get him down to the station," Rick barked to the cop standing behind Jimmy.

Rick turned and walked back toward his patrol car.

"What do we do with these other two?" one officer asked.

Rick turned back toward Red and Dan and shot them a look of disgust.

"Un-cuff them and let them go."

The officer bent down to release the cuffs.

You're both lucky I don't arrest you," Rick said to Dan.

Dan stood up, rubbing his wrists. "For what?"

"Obstruction of justice, aiding and abetting, interference in an ongoing investigation, practicing without a license … should I go on?" Rick said, turning back toward his car.

"We should arrest him for being a dick," Red said.

Chapter Twenty One

Dan pulled his Porsche into Red's parking lot, with Red in his Jeep right behind him. The two came to a stop side by side across the parking lot from the front doors. Red turned off his engine, which also ended Billy Idol's "White Wedding." Billy may have stopped singing, but Red didn't. Dan looked over and shook his head. Red had the voice of a bird, but not a song bird, more like a pterodactyl.

"Wow," Red said after mercifully ending his performance, "did you see the look on Carver's face? Man, he was pissed at you."

"Yeah, he thinks we're friends. Hates it when I go behind his back on something like this. He acts like a chick that's just found out she's been cheated on."

Dan reached for the door, opened it, and motioned for Red to enter first.

"You're such a gentleman, Coast."

Red walked behind the bar. Dan climbed up on a stool and rested his forearms on the bar.

"Tequila—"

"Seven, and lime. I know, I know." Red reached under the bar and pulled out two rocks glasses, scooped them into the ice maker, and set them on the bar side by side. A shot of tequila in Dan's glass and a shot of whiskey in his own. Red reached for the soda gun, pressed the one marked 7UP. It spit and sputtered. He looked up at Dan.

"Ginger ale okay? The 7UP's empty."

Dan waived an indifferent hand. "Sure, that's fine."

Red finished the drink and slid it over to Dan. Dan downed it and slid it back for another.

"Put it on my tab," Dan said.

Red made another, slid it back, and then sat on a stool behind the bar.

"What's next?" Red asked.

Dan didn't have time to answer as Jock the cook came through the kitchen door.

"What's up, Boss?" Jock asked. He headed to the soda gun and filled himself a glass of water.

Dan always thought Jock looked like Lou Ferrigno, TV's Hulk, gone to pot. The man had flabby biceps you could show a movie on, and if you braided the hair in his nose together, you could skip rope. His unappetizing appearance and questionable hygiene aside, he was an amiable bloke, and Dan liked him. Plus, he made a mean club sandwich.

"Not much, Jocko. Any sign of Cindy today?" Red asked.

"Naw. She never came in, and she never called. Derrick called twice this morning looking for her."

"Sound pissed?" Red asked.

"Naw, he sounded more worried than pissed. Said he hadn't seen her in two days. He was wondering if anyone here had heard from or seen her. No one had, I told him. I asked him if he had called the police. He said no. I told him maybe he should. Then he hung up on me."

"She stayed at Bev's two nights ago," Dan put in. "Maybe she stayed there again last night. I'll go over and check when I get home."

Red added, "Make sure you stop by Phil's place on the way home and grab Jimmy's gun outta the boat."

"Shit, that's right!" Dan downed the last of his drink and slid his glass back to Red a second time. "One more for the road."

"Let me guess. On your tab?"

Chapter Twenty Two

Dan got out of his car and walked down the gravel pathway to his backyard. He was carrying Jimmy's pistol in a brown paper bag. He walked up his steps, put his hand on the doorknob, and paused. *Deja-vu.* He looked over toward Bev's. Buddy was lying on her small back deck, sunning himself. *If I had a deck, I wonder if that mutt would lay over here?* Dan thought.

Dan walked toward Bev's. When he got to her steps, she was walking out of her door.

"Hey, Dan. I thought I heard you pull in."

"You did."

They each took a seat on one of Bev's deck chairs.

"Chief Carver stopped over this morning," Bev said.

"What did he have to say?"

"I did most of the saying, he did most of the asking."

"You're a real chatterbox today, aren't you, Bev?" said Dan a little peevishly. "What did he have to ask?"

"He knocked on your door first. Then he knocked on Edna McGee's door. When he didn't get an answer, he came over here. He wanted to know where you were, what time you left. Things like that."

"And what did you tell him?" Dan asked.

"Told him I didn't notice," Bev said, grinning. "Then most of his questions were about Paula. What time I saw her last? Did I see her leave? And of course, did I see anyone over there?"

"And what did you say?"

"I told him the truth, Dan. I told him I saw Derrick leaving your house a little while before you came home."

"How did he react?"

"With that same smirk he always has. That 'I know something you don't know, because I'm so smart and you're so stupid,' smirk. Just kept writing in that stupid note pad of his, like he's some kind of super sleuth or something."

Dan imitated the smirk, pretending the palm of his hand was a note pad, and his finger was a pencil.

"That's the one!" Bev chortled.

Dan laughed along with her.

"Did you see the morning paper?" he asked.

"Yes. You want to look at it?"

"Sure. Grab it when you go in and make me a drink."

"Yeah, I'll do that while you're building a fire."

They both got up at the same time. Bev went toward the door, Dan toward the steps. Dan looked down at Buddy.

"Come on boy!" he said, slapping the side of his leg.

Buddy got up, looked at Dan, then at Bev.

Dan frowned. "Come on Boy! You don't need her permission."

Bev opened her screen door, walked inside, and held the door for Buddy. He followed her in.

"Goddamn dog," Dan said under his breath.

Chapter Twenty Three

Dan sat on his wooden Adirondack chair, leaning forward, arms outstretched toward the fire to warm his hands. It was getting cooler out now that the sun had gone down. He looked out toward the beach at the picture postcard view. The full moon, reflecting on the gently lapping evening tide. A couple walked along with a small boy, maybe five, and a dog on a leash. The father chased the child with a stick he had picked up, pretending to spank him as they ran along. The dog barked, wanting to join the fun. The mother laughed out loud. Dan stared, sat back in his chair, and sighed.

"Frank and I always said we'd wait for the right time to have children," Bev said, as she walked up behind Dan's chair. She handed him a drink, and put her hand on his shoulder. "Maybe after Frank got out of the service. Maybe after we saved up a little more money. Time got away from us. After a while we had waited too long. Looking back now, I wish we hadn't of waited. It would be nice to have a part of Frank here in the world with me. Someone that knew him, someone to carry on his name."

"I know just what you mean, Bev."

Bev walked over and sat down in the other chair. The two of them watched the family stroll down the beach, the parents idly picking up shells while the boy played fetch with the eager dog. Neither said a word till they were out of sight. Dan took a big swig of his drink and swallowed it quick. No glass was large enough.

"So, I suppose Rick has an all-points bulletin out for Derrick," Bev said.

"I would imagine so," Dan answered. "But he also arrested Jimmy Pantucco this afternoon."

"What does he think, Derrick and Pantucco teamed up and killed Paula?" Bev marveled. She shook her head and sipped her drink.

"Who knows what he's thinking. Oh, that reminds me. I forgot to ask you, have you seen Cindy today?"

"No. Not since she stayed here the other night."

"She hasn't been into work for a couple of days. Derrick keeps calling Red's looking for her."

Bev stretched her legs and took a swat at a mosquito. "Well, ya know, that old boyfriend of hers, Mark, was on the island. He's staying at the Leonards' place. I think he was supposed to leave yesterday. I wonder if she left with him?"

"You think she would have told someone. Said good-bye or something."

"Maybe someone should call Chicago and talk to her parents. Maybe she's there, or at the least maybe they know where she is."

"Good idea," Dan agreed. "I have their number somewhere. Her father gave it to me when he first came down here to see why Cindy never came home from spring break. We talked a lot. He asked me to keep an eye on her. To call him if she was ever in trouble."

"This might be a good time to call."

"Yeah, I'll call first thing in the morning."

The fire was dying down; Dan and Bev's glasses were empty.

"Should I throw some more wood on the fire and make a couple more drinks?" Dan asked.

"I don't think so, hon," Bev answered, stretching. "I better get on in the house and get to bed."

Bev got up out of the chair with a groan, walked back across the yards to her house. Buddy was waiting by the back door.

"Call your dog, Dan," she hollered.

"No," Dan yelled back.

He stood up and tossed the little bit of water in his glass into the fire. It hissed and there was a little smoke but it didn't put out the small flames that were left. He gave a quick look around, unbuttoned his fly and finished the job.

Chapter Twenty Four

"Hey, you alive?"

Dan opened his eyes. He opened and closed them a few times, trying to get them to focus. It hurt just to open them. His head pounded with every heartbeat. He was sitting in his chair. The almost full bottle of Scotch that had been sitting on the dining room table was now sitting empty on the floor beside Dan's chair.

The blurry figure of a stocky man was standing between Dan and his television with the remote control in his hand. His back was to Dan, and he was surfing the channels.

"Goddamn *Today Show*, *TMZ*, who the hell cares who Jennifer Aniston is banging, or what third world country Madonna is stealing her next kid from? I just can't watch this shit," The man complained. He shut off the television, turned, and tossed the remote into Dan's lap. "Christ, you look like shit. You drink that whole bottle yourself?"

"Most of it. How did you get out of jail, Jimmy?"

"I ex-caped. Overpowered the guard, took his gun from him, and hid in the laundry truck."

"Sounds like you've been watching too much TV, Jimmy."

"All right, all right, they let me go. The chief called my bar and the employees told him I was there all day the day Paula was killed. Also, they caught that skinny little *moulinyan* late last night. They're thinking he might have done it."

"Derrick? Why the hell would Derrick have killed Paula?"

"Who knows? He probably came in to steal your TV or something, and Paula walked in and caught him, so he killed her. Who knows why any of *those people* do anything they do."

"You're an asshole Jimmy, ya know that. It doesn't make sense. Derricks a good kid. If he was here there was a reason … and it wasn't to steal my TV, ya dick."

Just then there was a knock at Dan's front door, and Red walked in.

"Hey! Did ya hear the news? They arrested Derrick White this morning." Red reported. "Oh, I guess you did," he added seeing Jimmy standing in front of him.

"Yeah he heard," Jimmy said. "I told him the good news a few minutes ago."

Red snorted. "Good news, my ass. He's a friend of ours, Jimmy."

"Yeah, well, he's no friend of mine. The goddamn *moulie* killed my wife remember? So it's *good* news to me."

"He didn't kill your wife, Pantucco," Dan said. "They got the wrong guy. Just because he was here doesn't mean he killed her."

"What the hell is wrong with you?" Jimmy exploded. "You don't think I did it. You don't think White did it. Are ya thinking its suicide? Do ya think she bashed in her own skull and tied a bag around her head? He was the only one spotted going in and out of the house. The chief of police arrested him. Open and shut case."

Dan's inclination was to bash in Jimmy's head with the remote, but then he would have to get up every time he wanted to change the channel. "Red, can you give this racist prick a ride back to the marina," he said, "so he can pick up his car and get back to Miami? I got a few phone calls to make, and I want to head over to Derrick's mother's house and talk to her. Besides, I'm sure he has to make funeral arrangements for his wife and get started on some serious mourning." He glared at Jimmy and added sarcastically, "After all he just lost the love of his life."

"I think I warned you about that smart mouth of yours, pal," Jimmy responded, pointing his stubby finger at Dan. His menacing look wasn't convincing.

"I haven't had breakfast yet," Red hinted.

"Yeah, me either," said Jimmy. "Let's hit a diner. I'll buy."

Red never turned down an offer of a free meal, even from a gangster.

"What's good around this little island of yours, pal?" said Jimmy, putting his arm around Red's shoulders.

Dan looked on in disgust, thinking, *I bet Red would have toasted free marshmallows at Joan of Arc's burning feet*

Chapter Twenty Five

Rinsing the shampoo from his head, Dan paused for a second, removed his head from beneath the shower head, and listened. Yes, just as he thought, it was his cell phone ringing. Quickly reaching down, he shut off the water and slid back the curtain. Reaching for the cell with his wet hands, he lost his grip and it clattered to the tile floor. The back separated from the front, and the battery slid across the room, coming to rest against the far wall.

"Goddammit!" he yelled, climbing from the shower and gathering up the parts.

After reassembling the phone and searching his call log, he pressed the most recent incoming call. An authoritative voice immediately began speaking.

"Coast? It's Frank Leonard. I've been trying to reach my daughter for two days. I've left messages on her home machine, as well as her cell. She hasn't gotten back to me. I called her work. The cook said she hasn't been into work for two days, and no one has seen her. Then I find out there was a murder … in your house. What's going on down there, Coast? Where's my daugh—"

"Slow down, Leonard. I know as much as you do. I was going to call you this morning to see if they had gone back to Chicago."

"They? Who's they, Coast?"

"Her and that old boyfriend of hers, Mark something-o-rather,"

"Mark, you mean Mark Foster? What the hell is he doing down there?"

"I'm not sure. I didn't get the whole story. I guess he's staying at your beach house. Someone said she was staying there with him."

Frank was apoplectic. "What's that little bastard doing at my beach house? I fired that son of a bitch three weeks ago. We found out that he had been stealing money from my company for almost a year. Over three hundred thousand, we figure. It took us a few months to nail him. I had to hire a private investigator. He blew everything on drugs and booze. The kid's no good. You gotta find her, Coast. I'll be on the next plane down." *Click.*

Dan dried off and got dressed. He called Red.

"Hey, Red, meet me at Leonard's summer place. I just got off the phone with Cindy's father. Something's wrong. That Mark kid wasn't supposed to be staying at the house. Leonard's on his way down here from Chicago."

"I'm still eating," Red said, his mouth obviously full.

"Just meet me there, Red."

Dan walked over to his night stand, opened the drawer, and reached in to retrieve Jimmy's Beretta 92FS 9mm Inox. *Birthday present,* he thought, and slid the gun into his waist band.

Chapter Twenty Six

Dan Coast took a left off of Roosevelt onto Hilton Haven Road. Hilton was a narrow road. He drove along slowly until he came to the Leonard's summer place. He pulled to the side of the road and parked when the house came into view. He turned off his engine and sat still, looking toward the house.

The Leonard's house was your basic Key West style home. It was two stories. The siding was wooden clap boards painted light green. The trim was the same color, and the wooden shutters were a dark green. The roof was steel and dark gray. There was a pathway made of red brick leading from the road to the front door. There was a short driveway, short but wide enough for two cars. The driveway was the same red brick. Red brick turned on its side bordered the path, the street, and the driveway. There were a few palm trees in the yard, scattered about in no certain formation. The sparse, patchy lawn was more mulch and wood chips than grass. Dan was certain Frank Leonard's lawn in Highland Park looked nothing like this.

Dan sat, staring at the house. He didn't know exactly what he was looking for. Perhaps a broken window, maybe an open door. *It would be nice if there was a sign on the front lawn that read, "Bad shit going on here, back doors unlocked,"* Dan thought. The house just looked like every other house on the road, however. Nothing special, nothing out of the ordinary.

Dan quietly opened his door. Reached back, felt for the gun, and proceeded toward the house.

He moved quickly toward the house, as quietly as possible, slightly bent at the waist, arms down at his sides. He didn't know why he should skulk around this way, but he had seen Thomas Magnum do it hundreds of times. He also knew that, more times than not a shot was fired at Magnum before he would reach his destination, and Dan was wondering if he himself would be able to drop and roll behind a bullet proof object. After all there was no stuntman to take his place, no director to yell cut, and there would be no take two.

He reached the front door without incident. Only then did he come to the reality that it wasn't even noon yet, and he was trying to sneak up on a house in broad daylight.

Dan pushed the doorbell button. He heard nothing. Was it broken, he thought, or was the bell maybe too far from the front door to be heard from outside? He pulled back the large knocker mounted on the door and slightly banged it three times against the brass plate. *That's some big knockers*, he thought and grinned.

He waited, listening intently for sound or movement from within. He put his ear closer to the door … nothing. *I wonder if you can really hear through a door better with a drinking glass? Drinking glass. I could really use a drink.* Dan reached down and quietly turned the door knob. It was unlocked. He pushed the door open a few inches and listened again … nothing. He pushed the door open and stepped inside.

"Cindy … hello ... is anyone here?" Dan called out. Loud enough for someone close to hear, but not too loud.

He was standing in the foyer. The walls were off-white, the moldings white. As far as he could tell all of the rooms were the same color. There was a closed door to his right. There was a doorway into a living room on his left. Straight ahead to the left of a staircase there was a hall leading to what looked to be a kitchen. The house smelled stuffy from being closed up for a while. It was dark. All of the shades and curtains were shut.

Dan walked cautiously down the hall to the kitchen. There were a few dirty dishes in the sink, a fast food bag on the counter, as well as a half empty bottle of Evan Williams, and two empty wine bottles. *O-ho, and what do we have here?* Three neatly lined rows of a white powder, lying next to a short silver straw, and a small bag of the same substance.

Hearing footsteps and what he thought were voices coming from upstairs, he turned and crept back down the hallway. Dan stopped at the closed door at the foot of the stairs and quietly opened it. He peered inside. It was an office. There was a desk and chair facing the door. Behind the desk there was a tall gun cabinet. The glass door was open, as well as a drawer beneath the door. A few shotgun shells were lying on the floor in front of the cabinet, and a few bullets were scattered on the desk.

Dan counted. There were six slots for rifles. Two were empty. Not a good sign. He started up the stairs. He was on the third step when he heard a voice.

"Why, *why* couldn't you have just come home with me? I didn't want it to be this way."

It was a male voice. There was no answer. Dan stepped on the fourth step, then the fifth. His eyes were level with the second floor. He could see into a bedroom at the top of the stairs. There was a young man Dan had never seen before. He was standing over Cindy, holding a shot gun. Cindy was sitting on the floor, leaning against the bed. Her hands were tied with a thin rope.

The young man spoke again. "Get up. Let's get down to the basement. I don't want anyone to hear the gunshot."

"Please, Mark, please don't do this," Cindy pleaded, sobbing. "We can work something out. We'll ask my dad for the money. You don't have to do this, please."

"It's too late. No more stalling. I have to do this now. If I wait too long they won't believe your boyfriend did it. They arrested him this morning for killing that friend of yours. They'll think he did this too, but I have to hurry or the time of death won't add up."

Mark was wired and speaking erratically, sniffing after every other sentence. His body language was very animated. Dan could tell he was on something: he'd probably hit that coke in the kitchen pretty hard. As long as Mark was pointing that shotgun at Cindy, Dan couldn't make a move. He waited patiently, motionless.

"I can get the money from my dad. Please, Mark," Cindy cried.

"No, no … this is better. They'll find your body in a few days. That insurance policy is still in my name. My money problems will be solved."

"It will never work, Mark. Everyone knows you were here."

"Yeah, that's right. Here because I loved you and wanted you back, not because I was going to kill you. Who do you think they'll believe, me or that black boyfriend of yours?"

He grabbed Cindy by the hair and pulled her up. The gun was at his side. Dan moved up a step. CREAK.

Shit, Dan thought to himself. He looked up. His and Mark's eyes met. Mark dropped Cindy and raised the barrel of the shotgun. Dan was amazed: the scene seemed to play out in slow motion, just like on TV. Dan could feel his own eyes widen as he saw Mark's do the same. Mark pumped the shot gun. Dan turned as Mark fired off a shot. The round ball at the top of the newel post exploded two feet from Dan's head, showering Dan's face and neck with splinters. Dan wrapped his arms around his head for some sort of false protection as he ran back down the stairs. Mark pumped and fired another shot. Plaster flew from the wall in small pieces, peppering the side of Dan's head.

After what seemed like an eternity, Dan made it to the front door. Before he could grasp the knob, it opened. It was Red and Jimmy.

"Look out, look out!" Dan screamed, as he heard the sound of the gun being pumped again.

Dan dove through the air, hitting Red square in the chest and knocking him to the ground as Jimmy quickly side-stepped out of the line of fire. The gun blast caught the edge of the door, slamming it closed.

Red and Dan scrambled to their feet and with Jimmy in tow zigzagged across the yard, searching for cover.

Chapter Twenty Seven

Red's Jeep was parked halfway on the lawn of the Leonard's summer place at the end of the long brick walkway that led from the street to the house. Dan, Red, and Jimmy were seated on the ground with their backs up against the Jeep's passenger side tires, facing away from the house. Red was picking small pieces of stone out of his bloody knee, injured when he fell on the walkway. Dan's arms were folded across his knees and his head was resting on his arms.

"What the hell was that?" Jimmy asked.

"That was Cindy's ex-boyfriend, Mark," Dan replied.

"He seems like a nice young man." Jimmy was brushing the bits of plaster from his shirt. He spotted a small hole under his left breast. "Ugh, this shirt is ruined."

"Screw you shirt! He's got Cindy upstairs in the house. I overheard him say he was going to kill her."

"Where did he get a scatter gun like that?" Jimmy asked.

"It's Frank Leonard's gun. Frank is Cindy's dad. There's a whole cabinet full of them in his office."

Red continued his self-surgery.

"Quite a coincidence," Jimmy remarked.

Dan glared at him. "What's that?"

"Two murderers on the island. I think this ex-boyfriend of Cindy's went to your house looking for Cindy, saw Paula standing at your sink. From behind they look a little bit alike. Bashed her over the head. When he realized he had killed the wrong girl, he set it up to look like someone else did it."

"Now *that's* detective work, Dan. How come you didn't figure this out?" Red said, while wiping his knee with a hanky he had pulled from his pants pocket.

"I must be an idiot," Dan said sarcastically.

"So, I guess that black kid didn't kill Paula," Jimmy said.

"White kid," Red corrected him.

"The black kid they arrested," Jimmy said.

"The black kid is the White kid."

"What White kid?"

"The black kid."

"How can the white kid be the black kid?"

"The black kid's name is White."

"Oh, so the bla__"

"Oh, for Chrissakes, shut up!" Dan thundered. "How the hell did I end up in an Abbott and Costello routine?"

"Well, ya gotta admit, that's pretty funny," Jimmy said.

Dan sighed in exasperation. "Yeah, maybe to someone like you."

"You mean a dumb wop like me?" Jimmy asked, grinning.

"Hey! That's racist," Red said, laughing along with Jimmy.

Right then a Key West police car pulled up in front of the three men cowering behind Red's jeep. The officer rolled down his window. Dan recognized the officer but didn't know his name.

"We had a report that someone out here heard something that sounded like a gun shot," the officer said.

"Yeah, exactly like a gun shot," Dan returned.

A shot rang out from the house, hitting the front fender of the patrol car. The officer quickly opened his door and dove to the ground at the three men's feet.

"What the hell was that?" he yelled.

"That's something that sounded like a gunshot," Dan answered.

The officer's name plate read *GUIDO.*

"Officer Gweedo, is it?" Red asked innocently.

"Now *that's* racist." Jimmy said.

"It's pronounced, *Guy*-doh," the officer responded.

Dan joined in on the laughter this time. The officer looked puzzled. He reached back into his car, grabbed his radio, and called for backup, as Dan explained the situation to him.

Chapter Twenty Eight

The standoff was entering its ninth hour. The sun had gone down, but there was still plenty of light in the sky. Four Key West police cars were now on the scene, as well as three Monroe County Sheriff's cars. There were two ambulance parked at the entrance to Hilton Avenue, and an emergency vehicle from the fire department was parked around the corner. Parked at the far end of the street was a SWAT van that had arrived pretty quickly. Six men had quickly exited the van dressed in garb that seemed to be a cross between police and military. The six men took positions around the property, and awaited instruction from a superior that stayed close to Chief Carver.

It was quiet now. There had been no contact from inside the Leonard house in over three hours. No lights or shadows in the windows. Gun fire had twice come from an upstairs window between two and three o'clock. No one was hit during either barrage, but it became clear that Mark had exchanged his shotgun for a high powered rifle of some sort. The seven holes in the side of Red's Jeep was proof of that.

The closest professional hostage negotiator was in Miami talking a future ex-husband off a ledge. Seems the man's wife had hired a PI to take pictures of him and his mistress at a quaint Miami hotel. To make matters worse, the wife then banged the PI in the same quaint hotel. The wife told her husband that sleeping with the PI was a big mistake, but she just wanted to get even with him.

Rick Carver was doing his best to negotiate with what little training he had in that field. He had sent in a pizza and sodas at four o'clock in exchange for a look at Cindy through the living room window, just to make sure she was okay, as okay as she could be with a distraught, coked-up, ex-boyfriend holding a gun to her head.

Frank Leonard had arrived on the scene at around three, quickly enough that you knew he didn't fly in with the regular folk. He was pretty upset with his wonderful summer home being held under siege. He was upset about the cop cars on his beautiful lawn. He wondered what the locals would now think of him. Oh yeah, he was also worried about his daughter.

Chief Carver picked the bull horn up off of the trunk of his car, fumbled for a small black switch on the side of it, and flipped it on.

"Mark … Mark Foster, this is Chief Carver again," Rick said into the speaker. He admired the authoritative boom the device gave to his reedy voice. "I just want to make sure everything is okay. You have my cell number if you need anything, or if you just need to talk."

"You're da man, Rick. He'll probably come running out now," Dan said walking up behind Rick with Red at his side.

"What are you still doing here?" Rick demanded.

"The roads are all blocked. Besides, Cindy's a friend of ours. If there's anything Red or I can do to help, let me know."

Rick spat in the dirt. "Shit, Coast, what could you possibly do to help? Somehow this is probably your fault. Just let the professionals handle this."

"Professionals?" Dan said, shaking his head. *Since when was an ape with a bullhorn a professional?*

Dan turned to speak to Red, but he was no longer at his side. Dan stretched his neck and looked around for his friend. He spotted him next to one of the ambulances, trying to talk a cute little red-headed EMT into taking a look at his injured knee. Dan walked over. The medic was cute all right. The closer Dan got, the cuter she became. Her dark blue uniform shirt was one size too small, even for an EMT with B cups. This one definitely had a couple of Cs packed in there. Every time Red spoke, she giggled. *The old pervert seems to be doing okay for himself,* Dan thought, but like any good friend, he moved in to cock block.

"I think he needs a sponge bath," Dan said. The young girl giggled.

"I just wanted her to look at my leg," Red said.

"Yeah, the tiny middle leg, I'm guessing," Dan said. The girl giggled again. Red was turning red.

Frank Leonard walked over to Dan and Red. He was dressed just as Dan had always seen him dressed: dark blue pin-striped suit, some kind of expensive Italian shoe. Dan couldn't remember what the name was, but he was sure he had heard Frank mention the brand of shoe at one time or another. Just like at one time or another he had mentioned the brand of suit, the brand of sunglasses, the brand of tie, the brand of shirt, and probably even his brand of underwear. Dan didn't care, so Dan didn't remember.

"I'm sure you boys are in desperate need of whatever expert medical assistance this obviously qualified young lady can give you," Frank said with undisguised scorn, "but if you can tear yourself away, I'd like to speak to you gentlemen for a few minutes."

The young girl was smart enough to know there was an insult in Frank's words somewhere; she just wasn't smart enough to know where.

"I'm qualified," she said, her green eyes snapping.

Frank smiled like a shark eyeing its dinner. "I know you are, sweetheart, and with those top two buttons undone, everyone can see both of your qualifications. Now run along and let the grown-ups talk."

The young lady's mouth dropped open. She spun on her heels and walked away as though Frank had just sent her to her room.

"I hope I didn't ruin either one of you gentleman's chance at playing doctor later," Frank said.

"No, Dan was doing a great job of ruining it for me before you got here," Red sighed. He turned to Dan. "Why do you always do that?"

Dan laughed. "I didn't want that girl to catch anything."

"Maybe you'll ... catch ... something," Red fumbled.

"Good one," Dan replied.

The three men walked across the street to stand in a neighbor's yard, away from the commotion. They were soon joined by Jimmy, who had spent the last few hours being questioned by the local cops, the county cops, and the state police. They all told him to stay nearby. Where would he go?

"Listen, Coast, you gotta get my little girl outta that house and away from that psycho," Frank said, dangling a keychain in front of him.

The blue fob, emblazoned with the Cadillac emblem, had three keys on it. Frank was holding one of the keys between his fingers.

"What's this?" Dan asked.

"*This* is the key to the side door," said Frank, waiving the key. "It enters a hallway underneath the staircase. Take a left and go down the hall to my office. There's a file cabinet against the wall behind the door."

"Yeah, I saw it."

"This is the key to the file cabinet." He identified another key with his other hand; it was the smallest on the chain. "Open the top drawer. All the way to the back is a Smith & Wesson .45: it's already loaded. Get my daughter out of there."

"These cops aren't going to let us just walk in that house, Frank," Dan pointed out.

"Let me take care of that." Frank said, looking over his shoulder at his rental car and grinning. "Go to the end of the street. Go into the neighbor's backyard. Go along their fence until you come to their shed. There's a small section where the fence is missing. It's right in line with the side door. Wait there till you hear the commotion. Then head for the door."

"What are you gonna do, Frank?" Dan asked.

"Don't you worry about it," Frank said. He turned and headed back toward his rental car.

"Let's go," Dan said to Red.

"I'll go with you," Jimmy cut in eagerly. "After all, this guy *probably* killed my wife."

"Go ahead, Jimmy," Red said. "I got some serious business to take care of over here. You guys be careful." He arched his eyebrows Groucho Marx-fashion and headed back toward the EMT.

Dan shook his head. Jimmy laughed out loud. Both men headed down the street. When they got to the end of the street, they turned back toward the crowd. No one was looking. They ducked into the neighbor's backyard. They went along the fence just as Frank had instructed. They came to the hole in the fence and waited.

Both men crouched down and waited in the quiet and darkness for what Dan judged to be ten minutes. Jimmy spoke first.

"I wonder what exactly we're waiting for," he said in a gruff whisper.

"I'm hoping we'll know when it happens," Dan replied.

Just then a loud crash came from the direction of the Leonard's front yard. There was a scream. Then there was yelling.

"Holy shit!" Dan exclaimed. "That must be it."

The two men headed for the door.

Dan quickly slid the key into its slot and turned. The door opened. Dan wondered how a snowbird like Frank knew which key was for the side door. Sometimes it took Dan three tries at his own front door, and he lived there every day, not just in the summer. They stepped inside. It was dark. They went to Frank's office. Dan opened the drawer. Jimmy quickly reached in and grabbed the gun before Dan had a chance to. Dan didn't care, he had his own gun. He didn't take it out. He didn't want Jimmy to know he had it unless it became necessary.

Holding the gun in a two-fisted grip, Jimmy glided through the house with the belied size and a confidence that showed on his face. Clearly he had done this many times before. Dan felt better knowing he was with a professional. As they crept quietly up the stairs, Dan noticed the little ball on top of the newel post was missing. He knew some of it was in his cheek.

At the top of the stairs, Jimmy pointed to the bottom of a door. Dan looked. There was light coming from beneath it. They heard sobbing and looked at each other. Dan stood on one side of the door, and Jimmy the other. Both men stood with their backs to the wall.

Dan whispered, "On three ... One—"

Jimmy hit the door on one, splintering the jamb. Jimmy hit the floor in a roll. Coming to his knees he fired four shots into a surprised young man's chest. Mark's eyes grew to twice their normal size as he stumbled backwards, crashing through the window. Dan reached around for his gun, but left it where it was. He grabbed Cindy and pulled her into his arms. Jimmy walked to the window and looked down at the dead man on the ground below. Three officers were already at his side. One looked up at Jimmy.

"Freeze!" the officer yelled.

Jimmy just grinned and stepped back out of the officer's view. Dan held Cindy as she cried.

Chapter Twenty Nine

Jimmy exited the front door of the Leonard's beach house first. His hands were in the air, and he was dangling the .45 from his right thumb. Dan came out with Cindy, his arm around her. She had a small blanket around her shoulders Dan had grabbed off the bed. Tears streamed down her eyes, leaving black trails of yesterday's mascara. Her hair was mussed and she was shaky as she walked. Cindy searched the crowd for her father.

Frank spotted his daughter through the line of policemen, who were now behind their cars with weapons drawn and aimed. He ran toward her, she toward him. Rick Carver's bullhorn-enhanced voice bellowed from somewhere among the police line, "Hold your fire! Hold your fire!"

Frank Leonard hugged his daughter. At that moment she seemed to be more important to him than his lawn, his beach house, and what the neighbors might think.

"Thank God," he said. "Thank God, you're all right."

"Daddy, Daddy," she sobbed, and buried her face in her father's chest.

Frank was still holding his daughter as Dan and Jimmy walked by. As they got to the road they noticed what had caused the loud crash. Frank had deliberately smashed his rental car into one of the ambulances to cause the distraction that allowed them to get into the house unnoticed.

"I hope he purchased the insurance," Jimmy said. Both men chuckled.

Two paramedics walked by, pushing a gurney. On it was a body bag, unzipped. Cindy watched it go by, and once again buried her face in her father's chest.

"How did it go? You guys okay?" Red asked.

"We're good," Dan said. "You?"

"I pick her up Friday night at eight," Red said with a cat-that-ate-the-canary grin.

"Can I get that ride home now?" Jimmy asked.

"Sure thing," Red responded, "if my Jeep ain't wounded too badly."

The trio looked at the bullet holes riddling Red's Jeep and laughed.

"All three of you assholes better be where I can find you for the next few days," Rick Carver said as he walked by them.

"Story of my life," Jimmy said. "Story of my life."

Chapter Thirty

Dan, Red, and Jimmy sat together at a table in Red's bar. It was crowded with the usual customers: college kids, a few sailors, some locals.

A large woman in her mid-forties was on stage, singing karaoke. She was on a mission to bring back skintight mom jeans, and curled up bangs, tsunami style. When she turned her head just right, you could make out a thick mustache none of her friends were brave enough to tell her about. She was working it. She was doing her best Tanya Tucker impersonation, belting out "Delta Dawn" at the top of her lungs. She sounded a little like Tanya Tucker, but looked more like Forrest Tucker. Her husband was at a table nearby. The stage lights were gleaming off his sweaty bald head. He sat facing the stage; his chair turned backwards, a bottle of Land Shark in his fist. He couldn't stop grinning at his lovely wife. At that moment he was the luckiest man in the room … the world, for that matter. The only thought in that shiny chrome dome of his was taking her back to their hotel room and going all Glen Campbell on her ass.

It was just before midnight. There were four empty beer bottles in front of Jimmy P., three upright, one on its side. He held a fifth one, half full, in his hand. A few empty rocks glasses sat in front of Dan and Red; various colored plastic swords were scattered about the table, as well as a few swizzle sticks. Dan and Red each had a full drink in their hands. Red was eating pop-corn from a red plastic basket. They sat there quietly as Jimmy finished his story.

"… so here I stood in front of this guy, I pull the trigger … and nothing. Gun's jammed. I look over at Tony and laugh. 'Gun's jammed,' I say. We look back at the guy; he's standing up from the chair, pulling a piece from his inside coat pocket. What the hell is an accountant doing with a gun? I'm thinkin'. Tony goes for his piece under his arm, panics, don't unsnap the holster. He's yankin' on the gun. The accountant starts shootin'. Me and Tony's dancing around like a coupla those town drunks in an old Western. The guy empties the gun, all fifteen shots … standing four feet in front of us. The gun's empty, he's still pulling the trigger__, click, click, click. We're looking at ourselves and each other. Nothing. Not one bullet hits us. We start laughing, the accountant's just standing there. I start doing this impression of Tony. I'm swingin' my arms around like I'm being attacked by a swarm of killer bees or something. Tony's laughing hysterically. We look over and the accountant's laughing too. Christ, that was one of the funniest things I ever seen."

Red's eyes goggled with intense interest. "Did you let the accountant go?"

"Naw," Jimmy replied hysterically. "Tony took out his piece and put one right through the guys' left eye."

"Good times, good times," Dan said sarcastically.

"Kinda makes our fishing stories sound pretty lame," Red said.

"I got a million of 'em," Jimmy said. "But if I told ya any more, I'd have to kill ya."

He laughed at his own joke. Dan and Red didn't. They just hoped it was a joke, and Jimmy had made up the story.

"So, which one of you Jamokes is gonna take me home tomorrow … and where am I gonna stay tonight?" Jimmy asked.

"Well … you can stay at my house tonight if you want," Dan said a little tentatively, drumming his fingers on the tabletop, "but if ya want me to give you a ride home tomorrow it'll have to wait till around three. I have to meet with a client tomorrow at noon."

"I can take you home in the morning, Jimmy," Red spoke up. "I'll just have to borrow a car, since mine was killed in action tonight. I'll pick you up at nine; we'll go finish that breakfast we started this morning."

"Thanks, Red," Jimmy said. He stood and headed toward the bathroom, adding, "I gotta go see a man about a whore."

"Isn't it, 'see a man about a horse'?" Dan whispered as Jimmy walked away.

"Whore sounds funnier," Red opined.

"'Whore sounds funnier' … 'I can give you a ride home' … 'We can finish breakfast together … Why can't you solve crimes like Jimmy?'" Dan said, imitating some of Red's fawning phrases of late. "Christ, are ya falling in love with Jimmy or what?"

Red snorted. "Aw, you're just jealous because he figured out who killed Paula and you didn't … and because he's a lot funnier than you."

Dan got up from his chair and shot Red a sarcastic look. "No, Red, I'm jealous because I wish I was your boyfriend instead of Jimmy. Tell Jimmy I'm waiting for him in the car. Make sure you give him a kiss goodnight."

"Dickhead," Red said as Dan headed for the door.

"Corn-holer," Dan said over his shoulder.

Chapter Thirty One

Dan pulled his Porsche into his driveway. He and Jimmy exited the car. Dan looked across the street toward Mrs. McGee's house. She had the drapes pulled back and was looking out her front window. Jimmy looked over and saw her too. Pointing his finger at her as though it were a gun, he let his thumb drop and faked recoil. She let the drapes drop back in place.

"Nosey old bat," Jimmy said. "She always looking out her window like that?"

"Always," Dan said. "She never misses a thing."

Jimmy squinted his eyes. Still staring at Mrs. McGee's window he said, "Someday she's gonna see something she wished she hadn't."

"She's harmless."

"Yeah, harmless. Someone might want to explain to her what curiosity does to cats."

Dan shrugged as they walked toward the house. "She seems like a nice lady. She bakes me Christmas cookies every year."

Inside, Dan made them each a Scotch and water on the rocks and then turned on the TV. Dan plopped down in his well-worn La-Z-Boy, remote in hand. He flipped channels, stopping at a Dragnet 1967 episode on Antenna TV. He'd seen it a million times. He watched anyway.

"That Jack Webb cracks me up. He's got all the personality of a cement block," Jimmy said, sliding a dining room chair over and sitting facing the TV. He sipped his drink and tried to make himself comfortable in the hard straight back chair.

"You might want to think about getting another chair," Jimmy said, adjusting his ample ass.

"I don't get a lot of company," Dan said.

"Ya got a dog?" Jimmy asked, motioning toward Buddy's bed.

"No."

"What's the dog bed for then?"

"My wife's dog sleeps there."

"Oh, yeah. The dog that killed her."

"Yeah, that one."

"I guess we're both just a couple of widowers."

"I guess we are."

"Ya think we should join a bereavement group?"

"I don't bereave we should."

Jimmy chuckled. Dan didn't.

Dan got up from his chair and handed the remote to Jimmy, and downed his drink. He fixed himself another Scotch on the rocks.

"Turn off the TV when you're done. Bedroom's down the hall on the left. I'm going to bed."

"Sleep tight," Jimmy said.

Walking down the hall, Dan took a slug of the Scotch and felt it pleasantly warm his insides. "I intend to."

Chapter Thirty Two

"Hey, what do you call a guy with no legs and no arms hanging on the wall?"

Alex stared at the self portrait of Vincent van Gogh. "I have no idea."

"Art," Dan said laughing. "Ya get it?"

Alex didn't smile. "Yeah, I get it. It's just not funny."

"Sorr-*eee*. When did you lose *your* sense of humor?" Dan asked.

Alex tightened her jaw. "It could have been when you kept making fat lady jokes while we looked at the Renoir. Or maybe it could have been your childish behavior while we looked at the Courbet paintings. Everything isn't a joke, Dan. If you didn't want to come, you should have just said so."

"Sorry, this just isn't my kind of thing. Jeez, they're just pictures. So calm down, for Chrissakes."

"I am calm, and I know it's not your kind of thing, but you could just try to enjoy it because I enjoy it. And they're not pictures, they're paintings."

"Sorry."

"And stop saying you're sorry. Just try an—"

*****

Dan awoke to the sound of voices, scratchy voices apparently coming from cop radio speakers. "Ten-four," one voice said. "Copy that," said another. Dan laid on his back, staring up at the ceiling fan. It was already hot. He was sweating. He wished the ceiling fan was on. He wished he hadn't made fun of the paintings. The sun was shining brightly through his bedroom window. He squinted and rubbed his eyes.

Dan heard more voices. He couldn't make out what most of them were saying. *What the hell is going on out there?* he thought.

He swung his legs over the edge of the bed. His feet landed on something furry. It was Buddy.

"Too much going on out there, pal?" Dan asked the mutt. "Ya know, some dogs might bark and wake a guy up if something was going on right out in front of his house. Lassie you sure ain't."

Dan looked out his bedroom window. He could see cop cars and several officers walking about. They were going in and out of Mrs. McGee's house. He quickly threw on a pair of jeans and a black T-shirt, and went out his front door. Jimmy was standing in the front yard, arms folded in front of him, facing the McGee house.

"What's going on?" Dan asked Jimmy.

"I have no idea. No one's said a word. Maybe the old bat had a heart attack or something."

At that moment the coroner's van pulled up in front of Dan's house.

"Looks like someone will be baking their own Christmas cookies this year," Jimmy said.

Dan didn't say a word; he just looked at Jimmy in disgust.

"What?" Jimmy asked, shrugging his shoulders.

Dan spotted Rick Carver and walked over.

"What's going on?" Dan said.

"Old lady McGee died last night. They found her in bed. Heart attack probably."

"That's too bad," Dan said.

"Ya mean too bad because you gotta make your own Christmas cookies this year?" Rick asked with a sick smirk.

"What's wrong with you people?" Dan asked, turning and heading back toward his front door. He walked past Jimmy, who was still enjoying the show, picked up his morning paper off the steps, and went in.

Dan threw the paper on the table, and went to the kitchen to make coffee. The coffee was already made. He poured himself a cup, took a sip.

"Good God!" he said, and choked down a second sip.

"Too strong?" Jimmy asked.

Jimmy had followed Dan into the house and was now standing in the kitchen doorway, holding Dan's paper.

"Just a little," Dan said.

Jimmy held the paper in Dan's face. "Did ya see the headline? TEN HOUR STANDOFF ENDS IN DARING GUN BATTLE. And look here: It says, 'Entrepreneur James Pantucco fired the fatal shots that killed Mark Foster, who had been holding his former girlfriend, Cindy Leonard, a waitress at a popular local bar and grill, hostage. Police credit Pantucco's heroic action with saving Ms. Leonard's life. Pantucco is in town in connection with the vicious murder of his wife recently at the home of Daniel Coast, a local playboy and amateur sleuth, but police say neither Pantucco nor Coast is a suspect in that case, the investigation of which is still ongoing.' Well, Coast, looks like I'm a hero."

"A legend in your own mind," Dan said. *He's a hero and I'm a playboy and amateur sleuth. What the Christ?*

"Hey, that's no way to talk to Florida's newest superhero," Jimmy said, grinning. "Maybe you and I should team up. We could be like those two guys on that old *Simon & Simon* show. What were their names?"

"You mean, Simon and Simon?" Dan asked.

"Yeah, those guys."

"We're not brothers, Jimmy."

"Those guys was brothers?"

"Yeah, Jimmy, that's why both their name—. Forget it."

Dan headed into the bathroom, closed the door, undressed, and got in the shower.

Chapter Thirty Three

When Dan exited the bathroom it was quieter than it had been earlier. He made his way into his bedroom with a towel wrapped around his waist. He walked over to the window. The cop cars were still there. The ambulance was gone; so was the coroner's van.

Dan got dressed and went to the kitchen for another cup of coffee. On the counter next to the coffee pot was a note.

Red came and picked me up for our breakfast date. Haha. Thanks for the drinks, the place to stay, and especially for the "daring shootout." I still owe you ten grand for helping me find my wife's killer. The paper may have said the investigation is ongoing but I think we all know that Mark Foster killed her. I'll be in Islamorada till the end of the week. Stop up.

Jimmy P.

Christ, he even calls himself Jimmy P., Dan thought.

Dan tossed the note back on the countertop, picked up his coffee cup and newspaper, and headed out the back door to his Adirondack chairs.

"Mornin'," Bev called out from her back deck.

"Good morning," Dan said, raising his cup in the air. Bev toasted back.

"Did your mobster friend head home yet?" she asked.

"Just left."

"In that case, come on over and join me."

"He's not a mobster, he's a hero. Didn't you read the *Citizen* this morning?"

"Well, I guess they couldn't print it if it wasn't true."

"Too bad about Edna McGee," Dan said.

"Too bad about her sister, you mean," Bev corrected him. "They say Edna will be just fine, just had some chest pains after all of the excitement."

Dan cocked his head. "What are you talking about? Carver said she was dead."

"No. It was her sister."

"Whose sister?" Dan asked, confused.

"Haven't you been listening? Edna's sister. She was in town visiting. She was in Edna's bed sleeping and Edna was sleeping in the guest room. Edna told Rick that she thought she heard a noise, so she went in to check on her sister. When she found her sister dead she pressed her own medic alert necklace. She went back in the guest room to get dressed. She felt a little faint so she lied down on the bed and must have passed out.

The paramedics were sliding who they thought was a dead Edna McGee into the ambulance, when the real Edna came walking out the front door to see what all the commotion was about."

"Holy shit! I would have liked to see the look on Rick's face when she came walking out the door," Dan said, grinning from ear to ear.

"Well, at least you'll be getting your Christmas cookies this year," Bev said.

Dan glared at her. "What's wrong with you people?"

Chapter Thirty Four

It was seven o'clock, Wednesday night. Dan Coast pulled off of Charles Lake Road into the parking lot of Red's Bar and Grill. Six cars were in the parking lot. One of them was Cindy Leonard's. *Why would she be back at work the night after such a harrowing ordeal?* Dan wondered.

Dan parked his Porsche and went in. Cindy wasn't there to work. She was there to pick up her paycheck. Derrick was with her, as well as her father. They were sitting at the bar, surrounded by the kitchen staff, a bartender, two waitresses, and a few customers. Cindy was telling the story as she remembered it. When Dan walked through the door she had gotten to the point in the story where Jimmy kicked open the door, dropped and rolled across the floor, and came up firing.

Dan knew it was the best part of the story, and Cindy told it well, but he wished it was him that had come in with guns blazing instead of Jimmy. He wished he was Florida's newest superhero. He walked up to the group.

"Here's one of my heroes!" Cindy said. She pulled Dan to her and hugged him.

Frank Leonard jumped to his feet to thank Dan and shake his hand. Dan grinned. He was a hero after all.

"All in a day's work, people. All in a day's work," Dan said, raising his hand above his head to hush the ever-grateful crowd of worshippers.

"Let me buy you a drink, Dan," Frank said. "What'll ya have?"

"Tequila, Seven, and lime."

"Get the man a tequila, Seven, and lime," Frank said to the bartender.

The bartender complied and slid the drink across the bar to Dan. Dan grabbed the glass and took a sip. The lime was a lemon, but other than that it was a good drink. Dan took another sip and set the drink back on the bar. He stuck out his hand toward Derrick White. "They let you out for good behavior," he asked grinning.

Derrick took his hand and shook. "I guess they figure Foster did it, so they let me go."

"Let me guess, Rick told you not to leave town."

Derrick chuckled. "You got it."

Dan quickly scanned the room. "Where's Red?"

"That's what we were wondering. I wanted to get my check before I left," Cindy said.

"Left for where?" Dan asked.

"I'm going home for a couple weeks. Derrick's coming too. We're flying out with Daddy early tomorrow morning."

"That's great," Dan said.

"Maybe I can even talk them into staying," Frank said.

"One step at a time, Daddy," Cindy replied.

"When did you see Red last?" Dan asked, addressing Jock, who he could see through the kitchen window.

"He stopped by early this morning to open up," Jock replied. "When I got here he asked if he could borrow my car for a few hours. Said he had to give that gangster hero a ride back up to Islamorada."

"...And no one's seen him since?" Dan asked.

Everyone in the crowd shook their heads, looking to each other for an answer. Dan was worried, but only for a moment. Red walked through the door. Everyone cheered.

"Another one of my heroes!" Cindy exclaimed.

Dan rolled his eyes. "What did *he* do?"

Red feigned a wounded look. "Hey, I kept that EMT busy while Frank drove his car into the side of her ambulance."

"And what a great job you did," Frank said. "Get this man a drink on me."

The bartender made a drink and slid it across the bar to Red.

"Thank you, kind sir," Red said, holding his drink up to Frank.

Frank tapped his glass to Red's and then to Dan's, and to a few others at the bar. Frank was a different man tonight. His daughter's life was saved, and now she was coming home.

"Kathy, slide a couple of those tables together. We all need something to eat," Red said to one of the waitresses while pointing at some of the empty tables. "And get that *jutebox* going."

"Where the hell have you been?" Dan said quietly to his friend Red.

"Worried about me?" Red asked.

"A little," Dan admitted.

Red grinned. "You old softie. Well, Jimmy and I stopped off at the marina to look at Paula's car. I mentioned I was going to need to pick up something cheap to drive while my Jeep was being repaired. He said he was probably going to sell Paula's Bug anyway. So he said I could have it for free. He just didn't want to deal with the memories. I took it for a drive around Marathon. It runs good, only a little over sixteen thousand miles on it. I said I'd take it. He's gonna meet me back at the marina tomorrow evening with the title."

Dan didn't speak. He just stood there grinning at the thought of Red's giant head and body stuffed inside a pink Volkswagen Bug, trying to get jiggy to the soothing sounds of one Mr. Billy Idol.

"What the hell are you grinning at?" Red asked.

"Nothing," Dan said. He downed his drink and asked for another.

By this time the tables had been pushed together and The Zac Brown Band were halfway through "Knee Deep." Cindy, Derrick, and Frank were ordering from the menu. Dan and Red walked over and joined them, just as Bev was walking through the door.

"Hey!" she said, "is this that hero's dinner I heard about?"

"Why yes it is," Red yelled out over the chatter. "Come on in, the liquor is fine!"

Bev made her way to the bar to get a drink. Frank Leonard held out his hand. "I don't believe we have met," he said. "My name is Frank Leonard."

"My late husband's name was Frank," Bev responded pleasantly. "My name is Bev."

"It's a pleasure to meet you, Bev." Frank's smile was genuine. Bev moved in closer. Cindy kept a watchful eye on her father. She knew with mother over two thousand miles away he could get himself into trouble.

Chapter Thirty Five

Dan came to in his chair. The TV was on. A silver-haired man with a great tan was telling Dan that the high for the day was going to be seventy-eight degrees, mostly sunny, but there was a ten percent chance of precipitation. The wind would be coming out of south at ten to fifteen miles an hour. Now the gentleman with his mouthful of freakishly white teeth was telling Dan to stay tuned after these brief messages if he wanted to see a dog that could water ski. Then came a douche commercial.

Dan reached for the remote. He wouldn't be staying tuned. He didn't care about waterskiing dogs, and he figured he wouldn't be buying any feminine products in the near future.

He got up out of his chair with the usual morning moans and groans and headed to his coffee pot and the aspirins in the cupboard. He poured yesterday's cold coffee into a cup and set it in the microwave on one minute. He opened the child proof cap on the aspirins with some difficulty and took four with a small glass of water. When the timer dinged, he reached into the micro wave and retrieved his steaming cup. Dan went to the cabinet below the sink, pulled out Buddy's food, and poured it into a bowl. Then he filled Buddy's water dish. As usual Buddy was a no-show at breakfast.

"Stupid dog," Dan mumbled under his breath, and moved to the bathroom.

Dan looked in the mirror over the bathroom sink. *Holy Christ*, he thought, *I look pretty rough.* He looked rough most mornings after a night out at Red's, but this morning he looked even worse. Something had kept him awake most of night, and when he did get a few minutes of sleep, he was having strange dreams. He dreamed about the grizzled old man on the porch at Sid's Beach Bar and Grill. He dreamed about fixing his wind shield wiper with duct tape. He dreamed about Paula's Volkswagen Bug. He dreamed about his wife's car accident. He dreamed about the drive to Key West from Islamorada with Paula. The dreams were odd, but by this point he knew what they meant and why he was having them. There was doubt in his mind about Paula's killer and last night's dreams helped him put two and two together.

He moved in toward the mirror to get a closer look at a spot on his fore head he had been watching for a few months. The spot was above his left eye near the bridge of his nose. It was discolored and oddly shaped enough to worry him a little.

Age spot or skin cancer, he thought to himself this and every morning when he looked at it in the mirror. He poked at the bags under his eyes. He took the palm of his hand and placed it on his head and pulled back to try and erase the three wrinkles that ran across his forehead. *Nope. They're there to stay.*

He glanced down at a glass sitting on the toilet tank. There was a small amount of water in the bottom of the glass. Dan remembered carrying the glass to the bathroom in the early morning on a piss trip. He picked up the glass, swirled the water and looked back to the mirror. "You're getting old, Coast, but it looks good on ya," he lied to his reflection.

Dan walked back to the dining room to the small bar against the wall. He looked for his bottle of tequila. It wasn't there. He looked back toward his chair. The empty bottle lay on its side. It had rolled over against Buddy's bed. Dan grabbed the bottle of Scotch and added it to the glass. *Just to steady up*, he thought. He took a sip and walked back to the bathroom.

Dan closed the bathroom door. Hanging on the back of the door was the pink robe. He thought of Paula. He carefully stepped from the bath mat to the shower without touching the floor tile. *Watch out for the sharks*, he thought. He took another drink and placed the glass back on the toilet tank.

Chapter Thirty Six

The banged up blue Porsche pulled into Red's Parking lot around eleven-thirty. The weatherman had been pretty close. It was sunny, and it was about seventy-eight degrees. *Even a broken clock is right twice a day*, Dan thought, as he looked at the sky. He was wearing an old Bob Marley T-shirt, tan cargo shorts, brown flip flops, and gold-rimmed Ray-Ban Aviators.

He parked the car, reached into the glove box, and pulled out Jimmy's pistol. He held it in the palm of his hand, and felt its weight. Jimmy had told him that the gun was a gift from his father. Dan knew the acorn usually didn't fall far from the tree, but still wondered what kind of a man Jimmy's father was. An inscription on the barrel read: *Buon compleanno figlio mio.* Dan had no idea what this meant, but he was pretty sure it wasn't instructions. He put the gun back in the glove box, got out of his car, and walked across the parking lot.

Dan walked into Red's, took off his sunglasses and folded them, and hooked them into the front of his T-shirt.

He walked up to the bar and sat on a stool in front of Red who was doing paperwork.

"What'll ya have, pal?" Red asked out of habit.

"Tequila, Seven, and lime," Dan responded as usual.

Red made the drink as he had done a million times before. Dan sat quietly and sipped the drink as Red returned to his paper work. Occasionally Red would look up from his figures, and every time Dan was staring into the mirror behind the bar. He finished his drink. Red made him another. This time the drink came with a question.

"What's on your mind, Dan?" Red asked. "You seem like you're a million miles away."

"No. Just about eighty miles."

"What's that supposed to mean?"

"Nothing … maybe. Or something. I don't know."

Red shrugged his shoulders and returned to his figuring. Dan returned to his tequila, Seven, and lime.

"Red, what time are you supposed to meet Jimmy to pick up the title to Paula's car?" Dan asked after a long silence.

"He's coming here," Red said without looking up. "He's going to pick me up in his boat and run me up to the Marathon Marina where Paula's car is parked. He's gonna to sign the title over to me, then I'm gonna drive the Bug back here."

"You mind if I tag along?"

"Sure. It'll give me some company on the ride back."

Dan finished his drink and slid the glass back to Red.

"One for the road," he said.

Chapter Thirty Seven

"Who's in the mood for a shootout?" came the voice from Red's front door.

Dan and Red turned to look. It was Jimmy, of course. He was wearing a plaid fedora, a hat that might look foolish on most people, but it looked like it may have been made especially for Big Jimmy Pantucco. He had on a tri-colored *guayabera*, more commonly called a Mexican Wedding Shirt, with four oversized pockets and flower embroidery that he wore loose over tan cotton pants. *An outfit designed for mourning the loss of one's beloved wife, no doubt*. Dan thought cynically. Jimmy pulled the fat, unlit cigar from his mouth, and walked inside.

"Hey, Jimmy!" Red burst out. "What's up?"

Dan looked at Red and shook his head at his friend's new man-crush.

"First I need a drink__, vodka martini, dirty, with two olives__, and then we'll head up to Marathon and get that new car of yours," Jimmy said.

Jimmy walked up to the bar and next to Dan and slapped him on the shoulder. Dan wasn't in the mood, but pushed out a smile. Jimmy reached his hand into his back pocket, pulled it back out, and slammed the palm of his hand on the bar. He then lifted his hand to reveal an envelope. Written on the envelope in black marker was *Dan Coast*.

"What's this, Jimmy?" Dan asked, looking at the envelope.

"That's payment in full. Ten grand, old buddy. I told ya, 'Find out who killed my wife and there's ten grand in it for ya,' remember? Ya didn't think I forgot did ya?"

Dan stared at the envelope for a while, then took it and put it in his pocket.

"Thanks, Jimmy," he said.

"No problem. So what's new, old buddy?"

"Same old shit__" Dan started.

"__different day," Jimmy said, finishing Dan's sentence for him.

Red made Jimmy's drink. A few minutes later he made him a second one, and then a third. Red had a few Scotch and waters himself. When the men had drank to the point that they thought they could still safely drive boats and cars, they each had one more and headed for the door.

"You have the conn, Jock." Red yelled to the cook, who was in the back preparing for the evening's dinner crowd, and the three men went out the door.

"I gotta grab something out of my car, I'll catch up to you guys in a second," Dan said as he turned and jogged toward his car.

Jimmy and Red walked across the parking lot to a dock Red shared with a few other business owners in the area.

Dan leaned into the passenger side of his car, opened the glove box. He looked back at Red and Jimmy. When they were out of sight he reached into the glove box and pulled out Jimmy's pistol, turned, and placed it between his waist band and the small of his back, then pulled his shirt over the weapon.

Dan remembered pretending he was a cop as a child. He remembered putting his plastic pistol in his waistband. He remembered hoping that someday he would do it for real. Until a year ago he had never placed a real weapon there. Yet he had done it enough times since then that it was beginning to feel routine. Dan also recalled pulling that plastic weapon from his waistband and shooting bad guys dead. He had done that for real twice now. That part of it didn't feel routine yet, and he hoped it never would. He ran to catch up with Red and Jimmy.

Jimmy's boat was tied to the dock. The boat was a little bigger than Dan or Red would have expected, and a lot nicer. Jimmy's boat was a brand new thirty five-footer, fiberglass hull, with two big diesel engines somewhere down below. Red was impressed. Dan wondered how much Paula's life insurance was.

"Whaddaya think, boys? Just bought her," Jimmy said.

"Beautiful!" Red enthused.

Dan said nothing.

When the trio had climbed aboard the brand new gray and white, Monterey 340SY, Jimmy started the craft and pushed the throttles all the way forward. Dan and Red fell backwards into the bench seat in the stern. Jimmy guffawed while chewing his stogie. He was proud of himself.

At about six miles out Jimmy eased back on the throttles, and the bow came down. He swung the boat starboard, parallel with the Keys, and shut the engines down.

"Pretty smooth ride, huh?" Jimmy said to no one in particular.

"Pretty smooth," Red agreed.

Dan said nothing.

Red walked up into the cabin to look around; Dan followed. Jimmy walked to the back of the boat, sat down on the bench, put up his feet, and relit his cigar.

"There's a box of these Cubans down below if you boys want one. Help yourself," Jimmy said.

Red didn't have to be asked twice. He headed below for the cigars. Dan walked back out of the cabin, showing no interest in Jimmy's offer.

"Who pissed in your Wheaties?" Jimmy asked Dan.

Dan didn't answer. He just stood facing Jimmy.

"You got something on your mind, pal?" Jimmy asked.

"Yeah, I got something on my mind, Jimmy."

"If you got something to say, say it."

"It's just that … some things don't add up, Jimmy."

Jimmy jockeyed his cigar from one side of his mouth to the other. "Things? What kind of things?"

Red walked out from the cabin with the box of Cuban cigars. He saw the looks on Dan and Jimmy's faces.

"What's up guys? What's the matter?" Red asked.

"Your friend Dan here has a few questions for me," said Jimmy. He jockeyed his cigar again, more nervously this time. "He says things just don't seem to be adding up to him. I think he wants to play Magnum PI or something."

Red observed Dan's flinty stare. It worried him. "What's he talking about, Dan?"

Dan didn't respond. He just stared at Jimmy.

"Ask away, gumshoe," Jimmy said with a chuckle.

Jimmy flicked his ash overboard, returned the cigar to his jaw, leaned back and clasped his fingers behind his head.

"Well," Dan began. "First there's the mileage on Paula's car."

Jimmy took the stogie out of his mouth, examined the soggy butt, and reinserted it. "What about the mileage on Paula's car?"

"She told me there was 15,700 miles on it when the two of you left Miami. Then you drove it to the Marathon Marina ... so there should only be about 15,800 miles on it, but when Red test drove it he said there was a little over 16000. That's what would be on it if someone drove from Miami to Islamorada, then to Key West, to my house, and back to the marina."

"Maybe she was mistaken about the mileage," Jimmy said, grinning.

"Maybe," Dan said, "but then there's the matter of your drive down to my house to pick up Paula."

"What about it?" Jimmy asked. His smile had left his face.

"When I asked you if you were to the marina yet, you said, 'No, it's up here on the right.' If you were on your way to my house, the marina would have been on your left. It would only have been on your right if you were headed back to Islamorada ... after killing Paula."

"Good story, Columbo, but remember, I have an alibi. The chief called my bar. Everyone said I was there at the time of the murder."

"I didn't forget, Jimmy. I didn't forget that they are all employees of yours."

Jimmy leaned forward; his face had reddened. "Anything else?"

"Yeah. I also think you snuck out of my house and tried to kill Mrs. McGee. I think you were worried that she may have seen you at my house the day before. After all, she was always looking out that window of hers. I think you wanted to … what was it, Jimmy? 'Teach her what curiosity does to cats.'"

A fine sheen of sweat had broken out on Jimmy's forehead. "The case is closed, Dan, and your ramblings and assumptions aren't going to be enough to reopen it. So why don't you take that ten grand I gave you and go on about your life, and stop worrying about mine."

"You're right Jimmy, my ramblings might not be enough to reopen the case, but they may be enough to get Chief Carver to look into it a little better. Maybe Carver will get the credit card receipts. Find out what customers were in your bar at the time of your wife's murder. See if any of them remember seeing you there. Maybe with a little more intense questioning one of your employees will crack, and tell the truth. Which employee hates you the most, Jimmy? Maybe an autopsy will reveal pillow fibers in Mrs. McGee's sister's lungs.

Jimmy's face went pale.

"Yeah, that's right Jimmy, her sister. Edna McGee isn't dead. It was her sister that was killed. I bet when the chief finally questions McGee, she'll say she remembers a guy that looks a lot like you going into my house the day of Paula's murder. Why, I bet your finger prints are even in McGee's house somewhere."

Jimmy had heard enough. He stood up calmly, putting his hands behind his back. Dan mirrored Jimmy's actions, watching his face, his hands, and his movements.

Red stood motionless, his eyes going back and forth from Dan to Jimmy.

"I thought you didn't think I was stupid enough to kill my wife like that," Jimmy said.

"That was before I got to know you, Jimmy," Dan replied. "Now I'm thinking you might be that stupid."

Dan could feel himself grinning. He didn't know if it was his adrenaline, or fear, or the satisfaction of watching Jimmy unravel.

"I told you twice now that that smart mouth was gonna get you into trouble," Jimmy said. His upper lip was sweaty and quivering.

Dan had taken his eyes off the Mafioso. "I heard what you told me, Jimmy, and I think you might even believe it, but I think it's you that's in trouble."

Dan saw Jimmy's eyes widen, his shoulder tilt forward, and his elbow shoot skyward in a single blurred motion. Dan already had a grip on Jimmy's birthday gun. He brought it around in front of him, just as Jimmy brought his gun around and pointed it at Dan. Jimmy fired first, shattering the windshield behind Dan. Dan flinched and fired the Beretta, hitting Jimmy in the right shoulder. Jimmy fired again, hitting Dan in the left thigh. Dan sank to his knees, squeezing off another shot into Jimmy's stomach. The gangster dropped his weapon and glared at Dan with hate and disbelief.

"I thought you threw my gun over board," Jimmy said, choking. His teeth were bloody, and a small trail of blood ran from the corner of his mouth.

"I lied," Dan said, pulling himself to his feet with the help of a deck chair.

Jimmy coughed again, spitting up blood. He tried to come at Dan but his legs wouldn't move. His knees wobbled.

"She was just a stupid whore," Jimmy said, trying to smile.

Dan raised his weapon and emptied it into Jimmy's chest. Jimmy stumbled backwards over the stern and into the water. There was a split second of silence followed by a splash.

Dan hobbled to the back of the boat, and looked into the water. Jimmy slowly sank as the air left his lungs.

"Watch out for the sharks, Jimmy," Dan said.

Chapter Thirty Eight

Dan spent the afternoon of the shooting in surgery having a bullet removed from his thigh. A few hours after surgery, against the wishes of Doc. Biddle, Dan signed himself out of the hospital, only to spend the next several hours answering Rick Carver's long list of questions. Dan told Rick about Jimmy's confession to Paula's murder and that he was also responsible for the death of Edna McGee's sister, Trudy.

Around 9:00pm Chief Rick Carver held a press conference. He stood behind a podium next to the American, and Florida state flags in front of a blue curtain. He was in his glory.

It was now early the following morning. Dan Coast was on his knees in front of his bedroom closet. The leg of his cargo shorts were pulled slightly up his thigh to reveal a large bandage. A dark wooden cane lay at his side. The closet floor carpeting was pulled back and a large floor board had been removed to gain entrance to a hidden compartment.

Dan pulled a black duffle bag from the hole and unzipped it. Inside was a large amount of cash, and a photograph of him and Candi in a frame. Dan ignored them both. He picked up the pink robe that was lying on the floor next to him and placed it in the bag. He then picked up Paula's cell phone, turned it on, and tapped the photo gallery icon. He sat quietly and looked through the photos. He saw the photo of the WELCOME TO PARADISE sign. There was a photo of Paula and Cindy. There was a photo of Red standing behind the bar with a huge grin on his face.

He stopped at the photo of him and Paula. He stared at it for a moment, shut off the phone, and tossed it into the bag. Dan took the envelope out of his pocket marked *Dan Coast* and took out the ten grand Jimmy had given him. He counted out five thousand, put it back in his pocket, and tossed the rest into the bag. He zipped up the bag, stuffed it back in the hole, placed the floorboard back into position and laid the carpet back down.

He went to his kitchen, poured a cup of cold coffee, put it in the microwave, and set it for one minute. He walked to the front porch and picked up the morning edition of the *Citizen*, went back to the kitchen, grabbed his coffee. He looked at the clock on the stove; seven thirty-seven.

Dan walked out his back door and down the gravel path to the two Adirondack lawn chairs that came with the place and sat down in front of the fire pit. He leaned the cane against the arm of the chair and unfolded the newspaper. The headline read, CHICAGO MAN CLEARED IN MIAMI WOMAN'S MURDER. Next to it was a picture of Mark Foster, Cindy's ex. There also a picture of Jimmy. The caption underneath read, *Big Jimmy Pantucco*.

Red walked up and sat down in the chair next to Dan.

"I see you read the paper," Red said.

"Yeah, we're famous," Dan replied sarcastically. Red laughed.

"Coffee?" Dan asked.

"Yeah, I could use a cup."

Dan reached in his pocket and handed Red the five thousand dollars. "Here's your half of the reward."

"Thanks. It'll make a nice down payment on a new Jeep."

"Isn't that what you did with the last money I gave ya?"

"Yeah, hopefully this vehicle lasts a little longer than the last one. You have *breaktist*?" Red asked.

"No," Dan answered.

"Come on, I'll buy," Red said, as he stood from the chair and jammed the cash into his pocket.

Dan Coast stood with a groan and grabbed his cane, and together he and Red walked up the gravel pathway and around to the front of the house.

The End

Don't miss the next exciting book from Rodney Riesel.

A new city

A new character

A new mystery

North Murder Beach

A Jake Stellar Novel

Turn the page for a preview

Chapter One

A morning run on the beach is the best way to start the day. Well, maybe the second best way. We had started the day the *best* way and were now working on the *second* best.

It was a few minutes past ten in the morning, a little late to start a run. The temperature hovered around eighty degrees, and the humidity was high for this time of the year, the combo making it difficult to take a deep breath. When I looked down I feel the heat coming off of the pavement. My shirt was soaked through, and I was wishing I hadn't lost my sun glasses the night before.

A good long run can sometimes get rid of a headache but this morning it was having the opposite effect. What had started out as a mere inconvenient pang was throbbing with every beat of my heart. As each step pounded the pavement, I felt as though the front of my skull might explode, sending hunks of grey matter, shards of skull, and blood into the street in front of me. *Wouldn't want to slip in it and twist my ankle.*

I eyed my running partner, Bree, who was a few steps ahead of me. She glanced back and smiled. I managed a weak smile back at her. *Damn it*, I thought. She was showing no signs of fatigue. I guess that's what being seven years younger and seventy pounds lighter can do for you. *I gotta lose some weight.*

I wiped the sweat from my brow and slung it to the road, more puddled on my forehead almost instantly. I thought about taking my shirt off, then thought better of it. Not out here on the street where someone I know might drive by and see my man tits flopping in the breeze. *I gotta hit the gym.*

We always start our runs on the street and end them on the sand. This morning we took Hillside Drive to Seventeenth, and then took a left onto South Ocean Boulevard. I looked over toward Molly Darcy's as we ran by.

"We have to get over here for some of those wings," she said.

"Uh huh" was about all I could get out. Bree had read my mind. Those whiskey wings were awesome.

"You okay?"

"Yeah," I lied. "Some pain in my left arm. A little pressure in my chest and the right side of my face is starting to sag."

"Do you want to stop?" She giggled.

"A little further," I gasped.

We arrived at Eleventh Avenue and ran down through the public access to the beach and turned back toward home. We made it to Twenty-first when I had all I could take. I started walking.

I said, "That's it for me." I bent over and put my hands on my knees. The sweat dripped off my head making tiny little craters in the damp sand.

She stopped running too but kept walking. I looked up and watched her walk toward the water, my hands still resting on my knee caps, the sweat still stinging my eyes.

She looked good from behind. She always did. She was forty-one years old, but from behind she could easily pass for twenty-one. When I met her I thought she was the most beautiful women I had ever seen. Seven years later when we were married I thought the same thing. After being married for thirteen years nothing had changed. Her beauty still amazes me.

When Bree reached the edge of the water she bent down to untie her shoes. Bending over was a good look for her. She wore a pair of tight black running shorts that barely covered her butt cheeks, and when she bent over they didn't. She looked back at me. I was grinning.

"What?" she asked, forcing a frown. "Stop grinning like that."

"Stop bending over like that."

"You're a pig."

"I don't think you're supposed to call a cop a pig," I said. "At least not to his face.

She removed her shoes and socks; so did I. She faced the water, pushed up on her tip toes, and stretched her arms up over her head. The muscles in her back and legs bulged. She was in great shape. Bree was muscular, but not too muscular for her four-foot-three-inch frame. She had shoulder-length hair. This month it was brown with a little red mixed in. It enhanced her dark skin tone and dark brown eyes.

I flung off my shirt and tucked it into my shorts. My muscles didn't show as well as Bree's. They were there, but at forty-seven they were now covered with a thin layer of fat. With my shirt on I appeared to be in much better shape. I was just glad at this age to still be sporting a full head of hair.

We walked along the beach at the water's edge. The waves lapped in allowing the water to rise to our ankles before it receded. The sun was behind us now. It felt cooler by the water. I bent down, filling my cupped hands with water, and splashed it on my face and ran my fingers through my hair. My headache was finally disappearing. We held hands. We always held hands.

"How far did you want to walk?" she asked.

"I don't care. As far as you want," I replied.

"When do you have to be back to work?"

"The seventh."

It was the first day of my vacation. I had taken eight days off. I took about a week off every year at this time. It was a good time of the year to take a break. The spring bike rallies were over. College kids were done with their spring breaks. Most families didn't book their vacations this close to bike week so the next week was usually pretty slow.

I'm a cop, a detective with the North Myrtle Beach Police Department; violent crimes division. After graduating from the police academy in the Bronx I was assigned to the forty-eighth precinct, also in the Bronx. I was in a uniform for eight years before making detective third grade and another six years to make it to detective first grade. Five years later I was burned out and looking for something a little slower pace. North Myrtle Beach was just the right pace.

"Did you want to do anything, go anywhere?" she asked.

"I wouldn't mind starting every day of vacation like we did today."

"I'm guessing you're not talking about the run."

"No, I'm not."

"I'm not doing that every day. Remember, I'm on vacation too," she said.

"You're vaginas not on vacation," I replied.

"What's wrong with you?"

"You would be better off making a list of what's *not* wrong with me. The list would be a lot shorter."

"You got that right," she whispered under her breath.

"Hey, I heard that." She knew I heard that. "When do you have to be back to work?"

"I don't have to be back till the ninth."

Bree is a nurse, an RN. She spent fifteen years in the ER at Saint Barnabas, in the Bronx before we moved here. That's where we met. I was in a uniform back then, five years on the job at the time. She was in her first year of nursing. She was twenty-one and I was twenty seven. I had brought in some kid that was wacked out on something. I don't remember what. He had tried to rob a liquor store with one of those Rambo knives. You know, the kind with the compass on the handle, fishing hooks and water proof matches inside. Somehow he managed to stab himself four times without injuring anyone else in the store. The ambulance came and transported him to St. Barnabas; I followed in my patrol car. That night I took one look at Bree working in that emergency room, and for some reason she looked over at me. Our eyes met. She smiled. If there is such a thing as love at first sight, that was it.

I got Bree's phone number from a friend of mine who also worked at the hospital. I called her a few days later. It took me that long to work up the nerve. We went on our first date that weekend, a seafood place. Bree ordered chicken. We saw a movie after dinner *Under Siege* with Steven Segal. It wasn't her kind of movie, but she didn't complain.

"The ninth? What are you gonna do those two extra days without me?" I asked her.

"Those will be the only two days I get to rest." She laughed at her own joke.

"Thanks."

We walked all the way to the Twenty-Seventh Avenue access. As we made our way up the path, I reached into my pocket and pulled out the three quarters wrapped in a tissue I had brought to pay for the morning paper. I always wrapped the quarters so I didn't have to hear them jingle in my pocket as I ran. That's annoying. I walked over to the big blue metal box that contained the *Sun News*, put in my quarters, and pulled out the paper. I glanced at the front page, NORTH MYRTLE BEACH WOMAN FOUND DEAD IN HER HOME. I folded the paper and jogged to catch up with Bree.

I rarely read the morning paper, but it was something I enjoyed doing on vacation. I rolled up the paper and smacked Bree on the ass with it when I caught back up to her.

She said, "You have issues, Jake."

"I never said I didn't."

We walked up Twenty-Seventh to Hillside, our street, and down two blocks to our house at the corner of Hillside and Twenty-Fifth.

Our house is one-story; three bedrooms, two baths. The siding is beige stucco with white trim, and stone around the bottom. The roof is a dark brown shingle. We have a driveway off of Twenty-Fifth Avenue that leads to a two-stall garage and a horseshoe driveway off of Hillside. There are three palm trees between the horseshoe driveway and the sidewalk. The house numbers are on the wall to the left of the door, TWO FIVE ZERO TWO. Above the numbers is a sign that reads, "The Stellar's".

The Coast of Christmas Past
From the Tales of Dan Coast

Coast of Christmas Past is the third book in the Dan Coast series of books. Dan Coast is all set to spend Christmas just the same way he has every year for the past few years; alone and drunk. But when uninvited, unexpected guests arrive and throw a wrench into his holiday plans he is forced to sober up (slightly), and throw on a smile. Just when it seems nothing else could go wrong, a close friend is injured in what appears, to the police, to be a drug deal gone bad. Dan Coast and his sidekick, Red jump into action to find the truth while their friend lies unconscious in the hospital.

ISBN: 978-0-9894877-3-3

The Man in Room Number Four
The Dunquin Cove Series

When a mysterious stranger arrives in the small coastal town of Dunquin Cove, Maine it appears as though Claire and her young son, Mica's prayers have been answer.

But who is he, and why is he really here? Join Claire and her guests at the Colsome House Bed and Breakfast as they piece together the mystery of the Man in Room Number Four.

ISBN: 978-0-9894877-2-6

Ship of Fools
From the Tales of Dan Coast

Ship of Fools is the fourth book in The Tales of Dan Coast series and begins where Coasts of Christmas Past left off. Find out how Dan deals with the death of a young friend, while looking into the disappearance of a new friend's sister. Join Dan, Red, and Skip as they fumble their way through a new mystery.

ISBN: 978-0-9894877-4-0

Beach Shoot
A Jake Stellar Series

It's a beautiful Sunday morning in North Myrtle Beach and Emily Bowen, a wife and mother of four, lies dying on the beach. Jake Stellar returns in Beach Shoot, a new mystery by Rodney Riesel.

Beach Shoot is the second Jake Stellar book and sequel to the Amazon Best Seller North Murder Beach. In Beach Shoot, Jake finds himself teamed up with the most unlikely of partners, his nemesis and fellow detective Avis Lint. Join Jake and Avis as they piece together the clues in this thrilling new mystery.

ISBN: 978-0-9894877-5-7

Return to Dunquin Cove
The Dunquin Cove Series

Return to Dunquin Cove, the sequel to The Man in Room Number Four, is the second book in The Dunquin Cove series.

It's been almost six months since the day ex-hitman, Ben Dunning turned up in Dunquin Cove, Maine, not knowing where or who he was. He's lived a quiet, peaceful life in the small town, but now his old life is calling him back. As Ben plans a trip to Boston in search of his past, little does he know that trouble is brewing in Dunquin Cove. Two strangers have arrived with the promise of safety and security. Join Ben and the people of Dunquin Cove as they band together to prove they can take care of themselves and their town.

ISBN: 978-0-9894877-7-1

Double Trouble
From the Tales of Dan Coast

Shortly after Walter and Warren Bowman arrive in Key West in search of a sister they never knew they had, Warren disappears. With nowhere else to turn, Walter enlists the help of Dan Coast. Join Dan as he and sidekick Red Baxter search for the missing Bowman family members, while dealing with the fallout of an ongoing case.

ISBN: 978-0-9894877-9-5

When Death Returns
A Jake Stellar Series

Has a serial killer from the past returned to North Myrtle Beach? Jake Stellar is back in When Death Returns. Join Jake and his partner Avis Lint in this exciting third installment of the Jake Stellar series as they investigate a homicide that eerily echoes the past.

ISBN: 978-0-9971149-0-4

From Here to There: A Collection of Short Stories
Within this book is a collection of short stories I have written over the past few years. The stories were mostly inspired by trips I've taken, places I've stayed, and conversations I've overheard from Maine to Florida. Although these stories differ from ones I have released in the past, I hope you will enjoy reading them as much as I enjoyed writing them.

ISBN: 978-0-9971149-1-1

www.ingramcontent.com/pod-product-compliance
Lightning Source LLC
Chambersburg PA
CBHW051954220626

47052CB00004B/935